THE GUNSMITH

#92

THE
ARIZONA TRIANGLE

The Gunsmith by J.R. Roberts

THE GUNSMITH

#92

THE
ARIZONA TRIANGLE

J.R. ROBERTS

SPEAKING VOLUMES, LLC
NAPLES, FLORIDA
2015

THE GUNSMITH
#92 THE ARIZONA TRIANGLE

ISBN 978-1-61232-695-5

For more exciting
Books, eBooks, Audiobooks and more visit us at
www.speakingvolumes.us

Chapter One

As far as Clint Adams was concerned it was becoming fashionable for the United States Secret Service to send for him whenever they had a tough one that their best man, Clint's friend Jim West, wasn't available to handle.

"Doesn't the Secret Service have a second best man?" he asked Gloria Manners.

Gloria rolled over in bed and looked at him. Gloria was a lovely young woman who also worked for the Secret Service. She had helped Clint disguise himself when he'd gone against the Fast Draw League[1] and they had become friends. The last time he'd seen her was when the Secret Service had asked him to accompany a visiting Russian baron on a buffalo hunt that had turned into a hunt for a murderer.[2]

One of the more pleasant aspects of responding to the various summons from the Secret Service was spending time with Gloria again. Ostensibly, her job was assistant to the head of the Secret Service, William Masters Cartwright, a man for whom Clint had very little use. As far as *he* was concerned, they should have turned that post over to Jim West a long

1. THE GUNSMITH #64
2. THE GUNSMITH #74

1

time ago—except that West preferred to be a field man. Clint couldn't really blame him for that. Maybe there was something about a desk that would turn the best of men into a bureaucratic asshole like Cartwright.

"They don't have a second best man who's as good as you are," Gloria said, putting her hand on his chest.

He looked at her and said, "There's two ways I could take that, you know."

"Well, I haven't taken all of the Secret Service agents to bed to see if I can find one as good as you, if that's what you mean."

Clint had often wondered about Gloria and Jim West, since he knew what a ladies man his friend was. Not that he'd have minded. Gloria was a wonderful girl, but he certainly had no claim on her, and vice versa.

He pretended to think about that and then said, "I think I believe you."

She slapped him on the shoulder and said, "You'd better."

He did. He had no illusions that she waited around pining for him between visits, but he knew she wasn't the promiscuous sort.

"So tell me," she said.

"What?"

"Why *do* you respond every time he calls for you?"

"Well, to tell you the truth, curiosity brought me this time."

"Curiosity about what?"

"Well, it's usually a message from Jim that brings me here," Clint said. "This time the message came directly from Cartwright. I'll bet he had to swallow a lot of pride to send it."

"So you're curious about what he wants, huh?"

"And why the message didn't come from Jim."

She was silent in response to that and he said, "You wouldn't know anything about that, would you?"

"All I know is that Jim isn't in Washington right now. I guess that's why the message didn't come from him."

"Do you know *where* he is?"

"No."

He wasn't sure he believed her, but he decided not to press her on the subject. He'd find out the answer soon enough from Cartwright, in the morning.

This was Clint's first night in Washington. He'd been here many times and usually stayed at the Presidential Hotel. In the past he'd met some fine looking women in that hotel, but this was his third trip to Washington—counting the Fast Draw League thing—since he'd met Gloria Masters, and now he usually relied on her for female companionship. Of course, he expected to come sometime in the future and find her attached to some other man. That was inevitable. A girl as fine as Gloria would not run around single for very long.

Gloria rolled towards him now and kissed his shoulder.

"Are those the only reasons you came?"

He kissed her forehead and asked, "Are you fishing for compliments, young lady?"

"One certainly wouldn't hurt."

"Well then, the answer is no. I seize any opportunity to come here and see you."

She lifted her head, stared at him, then sighed and settled her head against his shoulder.

"I wish I believed that."

"Tell *me* something now," Clint said.

"What?"

"Isn't there a young man—"

"No."

"You didn't let me finish."

"There is no young man in my life at the present time," she said. "That's the question you were going to ask, wasn't it?"

"Yes."

There was an awkward silence between them then, and she finally broke it.

"As to your next, unasked question, no, it's not because I'm waiting for you. I know I can't expect any more from you than this, and I don't."

"Gloria—"

She slid up against him, mashing her breasts against him, and kissed him.

"Quiet," she said, "just keep quiet about that, all right?"

"All right."

She kissed him again and slid on top of him. He slid his hands down her elegant back and cupped her smooth, taut buttocks. She lifted her hips, reached down between them and guided his swollen penis until he slid into her smoothly, closing his eyes as the intense heat of her closed around him.

She rode him that way for a while and then he rolled her over and, with a small animal growl, began to take her in long hard strokes that had her grunting and crying out. He slid his hands beneath her to cup her buttocks again, enjoying the way it felt in his hands. She was a slender woman, but she had firm breasts and a fine, firm ass that was just about his favorite part of her—that, and an amazingly sweet mouth. Hell, he just liked her, period, from head to toe, liked her so much that sometimes it—well, it scared him. He only felt that way about one other woman in his life right now, and that was a lady bounty hunter named Anne Archer.[3]

Finally, Gloria closed her legs around his hips and pressed her sweet mouth over his, her tongue blossoming there, to muffle the scream that was welling up in her throat as her orgasm approached . . .

Chapter Two

Clint stayed the night with Gloria and then saw her off to work. After she left he had another cup of coffee in her apartment and then took his time bathing and dressing. He was fairly sure that Cartwright knew about his relationship with Gloria, but there was no point throwing it into the man's face by arriving at his office on C Street together.

Gloria had probably arrived at work at nine A.M. Clint ambled into the man's office around eleven, and Gloria—although Cartwright's *assistant* and not his *secretary*—showed him in.

Cartwright, as stoic and disapproving as ever when he was in the same room with Clint Adams, was seated behind his desk and did not rise.

"You could have come earlier, Adams," he said.

"You know," Clint said, "one of these days I'll get a message from you and remember your manners, and I won't show up."

Cartwright looked as if he had a reply right on the tip of his acid tongue but he surprised Clint by swallowing it back down.

"All right," he said, finally, "have a seat."

Clint sat across from the man, folded his hands in his lap, and waited.

"We're having a problem we think you can help us with, Adams," the man said.

"And that is?"

Cartwright stood up and turned to face a map of the United States on the wall behind him. He pointed to Arizona and continued.

"There is a section of Arizona that we are very concerned about, right here," Cartwright said. His finger stabbed just about at the center of the state. "In fact, the area we're concerned with, starting here at Mesa, forms an almost perfect triangle. The entire area covers a section of roughly a hundred square miles."

"And just what is the problem?" Clint asked.

Cartwright left the map and sat down at his desk again.

"In the past fourteen months a total of twenty-one people have disappeared in that area."

"What do you mean 'disappeared?'"

"Just that. They rode into that triangle section of Arizona and have never been seen again."

"Do these people have anything in common?" Clint asked.

"Nothing," Cartwright said. "Men, women, children, people from all kinds of backgrounds and professions."

"Have you sent anyone else in there yet?"

Cartwright's jaw clenched for just a moment and then he said, "Yes. Two of our people have disappeared, just like the rest."

"I see," Clint said. "And now you want me to go into that triangle and find them."

"Yes."

"And maybe disappear myself."

"That's possible."

"And you want me to do this in the name of . . .

what? Patriotism? Humanity? You want me to go where twenty-one people have disappeared without a trace and risk having the same thing—"

"Friendship," Cartwright said.

That stopped Clint.

"Come again?"

"I want you to do it in the name of friendship."

Clint couldn't believe his ears.

"You're invoking the word friendship between *us*?" he asked in disbelief.

"No," Cartwright said, "not between us. You're no doubt curious as to why this time the message came from me and not from Jim West."

"Yes, I am," Clint said, but he wasn't going to give Cartwright the satisfaction of having to ask him. He was glad the man had brought the subject up himself.

"Well, the first agent we sent into that triangle was a woman named Kate O'Hara."

"Kate!"

Clint had worked with Kate some years back when they'd gone after a phony holy man named the Reverend Wellfall.[4] She was a feisty young Irish woman whom he had come to like very much.

"That's not fair, Cartwright," he said, eyeing the man with intense dislike. "Did you send her in alone?"

"Yes."

"What the hell did you—"

"She's an agent, Adams," Cartwright said, "a trained agent. It doesn't matter that she was a woman."

"Is," Clint said, "is a woman. Just because she's

dropped out of sight doesn't mean that she's dead."

"That's what our other agent said, and that's why he went in after her."

"And?"

"He's gone, too."

In spite of the fact that it was Kate O'Hara who was missing Clint was still having second thoughts. She may have been a trained agent, but he certainly wasn't. At best he was a talented amateur with a knack for getting the job done.

"Look, Cartwright—"

"The other agent was Jim West, Adams."

That hit Clint liked a cold fist clutching at the inside of his stomach.

"Jim?"

"He insisted on going in after her alone," Cartwright said. "He sent me a message when he reached Mesa, and that was the last I heard from him. That was a week ago. When he turned up missing I sent for you immediately."

"Why?" Clint asked. "Why not send a couple of agents in there after them?"

"Who do I send, Adams?" Cartwright asked. "Who do I ask to go where twenty-one people have disappeared?"

"Ask?" Clint said. "You don't *ask*, man, you *order*. This is your department, isn't it? You're the boss? Or do you just enjoy *playing* boss?"

"I asked for volunteers, Adams," Cartwright said. "After two agents came up missing I thought that was the fair thing to do."

Clint thought it over a moment and then realized that it was an amazingly fair thing for a man like Cartwright to have done.

"Did you get any?"

"Yes. One."

"And?"

"I don't want to send a woman in there alone again."

"Another woman? You have another woman agent?"

"Not exactly an agent," Cartwright said, "but nevertheless she's volunteered to go in—with you."

"Jesus," Clint said. As much respect as he had for Kate O'Hara's talents he didn't relish going into this with a woman in tow.

"And who is this almost agent you're looking to saddle me with?" he asked.

"You know her," Cartwright said. "Her name is Gloria Manners."

Chapter Three

"You're crazy if you think I'm letting you send Gloria in there," Clint said.

"That's not your decision, Adams," Cartwright said.

"Like hell it isn't," Clint said. "If she goes you can send her alone because I'm not going with her."

"Is that how much you think of her?" Cartwright asked. "I thought you and she were . . . friends."

"We are," Clint said. "If you want me to go I go alone. If you want her to go, then she goes alone. You decide which way you've got the best chance of finding out what's going on in Arizona."

The triumphant look on Cartwright's face wasn't hard to miss, and Clint knew he'd been had.

Or had he?

"All right, Cartwright," he said, "I'm going. Now tell me, did she really volunteer to go?"

"Oh, she volunteered, all right," he said, "and I'm going to leave it to you to tell her she's *not* going."

Another shock for Clint. William Masters Cartwright had a sense of humor.

• • •

Clint and Cartwright took a few moments to discuss the conditions under which Clint would arrive in Mesa, Arizona. Cartwright thought he should wear a disguise, as he did in the Fast Draw League thing, but Clint disagreed.

"If I get caught and whoever's behind this finds out I'm in disguise, then they'll know I was sent in. I've got to go in as myself if I'm going to have a chance of cracking this."

"All right," Cartwright finally agreed, "but contact me as soon as you arrive in Mesa."

"Don't worry," Clint said, "I will."

"There's got to be another town after Mesa that has a telegraph line. Keep in contact with me as long as you can, from town to town."

Clint nodded and stood up.

"Find out what happened to those people, Adams," Cartwright said.

"Don't worry, I will," Clint said. "I'll get Jim West back here if it kills me. Without him, you'll always be sending for me, and if that happens I might as well work for you permanently."

He didn't miss the pained look on Cartwright's face as he left the man's office.

When he left the office of the head of the Secret Service he told Gloria that he was taking her to lunch.

"I'd better tell Mr. Cartwright—"

"He already knows," Clint said. "We have some things to talk about."

The look he gave her told Gloria just what they were going to talk about.

• • •

"I'm going," Gloria said stubbornly for about the fifth time in as many minutes.

"You're not," Clint said.

"Why not?"

"You have no training, Gloria."

"Neither do you," she shot back.

"I have other experience, though," he said. "All you've done is sit behind a desk—"

"I helped you with the Fast Draw League—"

"Yes, you did, but you did it from here. That's what I want you to do this time, also."

"What can I do from here?" she asked, pouting.

"You can be safe," he said. "That's what I need to know while I'm in Arizona, to know that you're safe."

Her face softened and she said, "Really?"

"Yes, really," Clint said. "I'm not going to be able to do anything if I have to worry about you all the time. Do you understand?" He hoped she would understand and not *mis*understand.

"I understand," she said, "but Kate—and Jim—they're both friends of mine."

"And mine," he said. "I'm going to do the best I can to find them."

"I hope they're alive," she said, reaching for his hands and squeezing them.

"So do I," he said, squeezing back.

"When will you be leaving?"

"Right away," he said. "There's a train west in an hour, and I'll be on it."

"An hour?" she said. "That doesn't even give us time to say—" The word "good-by" stuck in her throat. "Clint," she said, "what if you don't—"

"I'll be back, Gloria," he said, squeezing her

hands even harder. "Just believe that I'll be back."

She smiled, fighting tears, and said, "I'll believe it."

Good, Clint thought to himself, at least that'll be one of us.

On the train an hour later Clint thought about what he was doing. He didn't know what he would be walking into when he left Mesa, Arizona, but maybe he could find something out in Mesa before he left. He didn't like walking into something blind, and he knew that Jim West wouldn't have either, if he'd been able to help it.

West would undoubtedly have asked some questions around Mesa before leaving to ride into what William Cartwright called "The Arizona Triangle."

Clint was going to have to walk in West's footsteps, and hope that he'd be a little luckier than his friend had been.

Chapter Four

As Clint rode into Mesa he took in everything with a suspicious eye. Every man and woman was suspect until he knew better.

Clint had left Duke, his big black gelding, in Labyrinth, Texas, when he had gone to Washington, so he was riding in on a horse he had bought in Denver.

He'd taken a circular route to Mesa from Denver, riding first through New Mexico. He hadn't wanted to pass through the triangle without first going to Mesa, since that was the last place Jim West had been heard from.

He left his horse, a three-year-old mustang, at the livery and went over to Mesa's only hotel. Mesa wasn't a small town, exactly, but he'd been in plenty of bigger towns. Average would probably be the best word to describe Mesa—only it was on the tip of a very less-than-average section of Arizona.

He checked into the hotel, signing his name at the bottom of a page on the right hand side of the register. Halfway down the left hand page he saw the name James West, with "Washington, D.C." written next to it. Jim had apparently been very open about his presence in Mesa. How open Clint couldn't be sure, but there were times when it was necessary for agents of the government to announce themselves as such. West had worked undercover many times, but it was not a matter of course.

Clint signed the register and wrote, "Oklahoma" next to it. Oklahoma—before it had become Oklahoma—had been the birth place of "The Gunsmith," although not the birth place of Clint Adams. The reputation had been born there, many years ago. It was as good a place as any to put next to his name in the register.

He wanted to ask the clerk some questions about Jim West, but decided against it. If West had been open, Clint would be less than open about *his* presence in Mesa.

He went up to his room, sat down on the rickety bed and spread a map of the territory out on the bedspread. He got a pencil and, starting at Mesa, drew himself a triangle. The top left hand corner was in the middle of nowhere, while the right hand corner was right in the town of Lakeville, Arizona.

Leaving Mesa Kate O'Hara, Jim West and even he himself would have no option but to ride north through the bottom funnel of the triangle. It was only when the funnel spread out that he'd have to make a decision whether to ride northeast or northwest. If he rode northeast and encountered no difficulty, he'd come to Lakeville.

If he rode northwest and encountered no difficulty, where would he end up?

The last town he'd pass through that way was a small town called Midnight. The name was intriguing, but the town was bound to be a collection of clapboard buildings, nothing more than a passing through point.

Which way had Kate gone, and which way had Jim gone, he wondered?

He folded the map, left the hotel and went over to the Mesa Saloon. He ordered a beer and took the mug to a corner table with him. It was early afternoon and there were only about five or six other men in the place. He nursed his beer and tried to figure out his next move.

If he went around town asking questions he'd announce himself, as Kate and Jim might have. Kate surely would have asked questions, Jim possibly to a lesser extent. Either way, both would have announced themselves to whoever was behind the disappearances.

Someone in Mesa had to be connected with those disappearances. Before leaving Washington he had asked Gloria to get him a run down on all of the people who had disappeared. She'd managed to get him the list right at the train station, just before he boarded. He'd looked at it on the train, and he took it out and looked at it now.

There were nineteen names, discounting Kate O'Hara and Jim West. There was one family of three that he could see, a husband, wife and child—a boy —named Wilkins. Other than those three, all the other names were different.

Gloria had supplied occupations as well as names and last known addresses. There were no jobs or homes in common. Drummers, merchants looking for a new place to settle, farmers, a rancher, one gambler—a man named Hastings, who he had never heard of—and a retired lawman named Letterman. He frowned, but couldn't place the name. Retired could mean a lot of things.

Gloria had not been able to supply him with ages. He himself had retired from upholding the law as a young man, so Letterman could be thirty-five, or sixty-five. Either way—or in between—if Clint found these people—and found them alive—the man might be of help.

Of the nineteen, fourteen were men, four were women, and there was the little boy. He was glad that there were no more children. He didn't know what had happened to these people, but he was glad that there was only one child involved.

He refolded the list and put it in his pocket. It told him nothing about why these people might have disappeared. There was no common denominator. If he had more time he would have liked to talk to someone who knew each of the missing people. Maybe before leaving Washington he should have told Cartwright to have some of his people do just that. Maybe in talking to friends and relatives of the missing people they might have been able to come up with some connection.

He was trying to word a telegraph message in his mind, one that wouldn't give him away, when he was aware that someone had approached his table.

The first thing he saw when he looked up was the badge. After that he looked at the man. The sheriff of Mesa was a tall, slender drink of water with a big mustache, big, knobby-knuckled hands, and a scarred eye that was always half closed.

"New in town?" the man asked.

"That's right."

"My name's Nichols, Wade Nichols. I'm the sheriff here."

"Glad to meet you, sheriff. My name's Clint Adams."

"I know your name, Mr. Adams," the sheriff said. "I saw you ride in, and checked at the hotel."

"Oh?"

"I know *who* you are, too."

"Do you?"

"Yes," Nichols said. "Do you mind if I sit down?"

"No, have a seat," Clint said. "Can I buy you a drink, sheriff?"

"I've got one coming."

At that moment the bartender appeared and handed the sheriff a cold beer.

The sheriff took a sip and then wiped his mustache with the back of his hand.

"What brings you to Mesa, Mr. Adams?"

"Passing through."

"On your way to where?"

"Nowhere in particular."

"Just drifting, huh?"

"That's right."

"Which way?"

"I don't follow."

"Which way will you be going when you leave?"

"Well, if you saw me ride in you know I came from the south."

"That leaves three possibilities when you leave."

"Well, if I had to pick one now I'd say north."

"North."

Clint nodded.

"Any reason why I shouldn't ride north?"

"No, no reason at all. Why would there be?"

"You're asking the questions, Sheriff."

"I'm just doing my job, Mr. Adams," the man

said. "You were a lawman for a while. You know we got to keep tabs on strangers in town."

"I remember," Clint said, sipping his own beer.

The sheriff took one more sip from the beer, then put it down and stood up.

"Not looking for any trouble, are you, Mr. Adams?"

"Trying to stay as far away from trouble as possible is a hobby of mine, Sheriff."

"Not the way I hear it."

Clint locked eyes with the lawman then and said, "Well, maybe you hear wrong."

"Maybe I do," the sheriff said. "I hope so. Good day, Mr. Adams."

"Good day to you, Sheriff."

Clint watched the man leave and wondered if he *were* just doing his job, or if he were involved with the disappearances.

Chapter Five

Clint remained at his table and looked over to the bartender to order another beer. It was then that he noticed that a couple of girls had come on duty. One of them, a small brunette with small, round breasts and big, heavily made up eyes was staring at him. He cocked his finger at her and beckoned her over. She started for a moment, as if surprised that he'd noticed her, and then pushed away from the bar and came over.

Up close she looked older by four or five years, but still only appeared to be twenty-five. Her skin was very pale, and she was wearing strong perfume.

"I'd like another beer, please," he said to her.

"Uh, sure," she said. She took his empty and the sheriff's half-empty mug and returned to the bar.

Clint looked around and saw that the place was starting to liven up. Pretty soon a poker game would start up, of that he was sure. Some of these people lived for the moment when they finished work and could come to the saloon for the poker game. That's the way it was in almost every town.

Clint was trying to decide whether or not he should sit in on the game in the hopes of hearing something helpful when the girl returned with the beer.

"Thanks," he said, accepting it from her small hand. He paid her and added something extra for her.

"Um, would you want to go upstairs?" she asked him.

He thought the question was odd, because she was asking it pretty straightforwardly, with no hint of the flirtatiousness that usually went with that kind of a question.

"Uh, no, not right now, honey," he said.

"You say when, all right?" she said.

"Well—"

"And don't ask none of the other girls," she said, cutting him off. "It's got to be me."

"Well, I'm flattered, but I really don't pay—"

She leaned forward, her breasts almost falling out of her peasant blouse and said, "You won't have to pay," in a low voice.

That kind of offer was usually hard to refuse, especially when the girl was as attractive as this one, strong perfume or not.

"What's your name?" he asked.

"Angela," she said, "Remember, it's got to be me, all right?"

She looked so hopeful he didn't have the heart to say anything but, "Okay."

She nodded, then straightened and went back to work.

Within a half hour the poker game had started. He watched as four men who obviously knew each other took a table which was obviously their regular one and started playing.

For a while he was able to hear their conversation, which amounted to small talk, but eventually the place got crowded enough that he couldn't hear them.

He decided to join the game.

He was getting up when Angela hurried over and said, "You ready?"

Even a girl as comely as she was could get to be a pest. She'd asked him that question twice already during the half hour that had passed.

"I'll tell you when, Angela, all right?"

"Sure, okay," she said. "Sorry."

He wondered why she was so eager to go upstairs with him, for free. He knew he was attractive to women, but this was bordering on the ridiculous.

He walked over to the four-man poker game and said, "Would you gents like a fifth hand?"

They all looked up at him and one of them said, "Who-eee, fresh money. Set yerself down, Mister. I hope you got a lot of it to give away. This here looks like my lucky night."

"Quiet, Lem," one of the other men said, "you're gonna scare him away."

"I've got nothing better to do," Clint said, sitting himself down, "might as well lose some money to the hot hand."

"That's a fine attitude," the man with the hot hand said. "I'll tell you what, friend, you're the newcomer. You deal whatever game you like."

"Nothing fancy," Clint said. "Stud poker, gents."

For the next hour Clint won a little, and more than once folded a winning hand. He wanted to keep the men happy and talking, and taking their money was not the way to do that, although as badly as they played, it would have been easy to do so.

After two hours, though, he decided that these four men had little to offer him. They appeared to be nothing more than merchants and citizens who met here each night for poker.

Clint played another hour, winning more this time, and finally quit the game up a hundred dollars.

They were only playing dollar stakes, anyway.

"Well, gents, I hope you won't mind if I leave a winner," Clint said. "I rode in today and I'm a bit tired."

They didn't look happy about it, but none of them objected.

"Besides," Clint said, rising, "I've got someone waiting pretty anxiously for me."

They looked over at Angela and saw what he meant, and suddenly became more understanding.

"Still be in town tomorrow?" one of them asked. He'd been the man with the hot hand when Clint sat down, and although he'd cooled off the last hour or so, he was still a winner.

"Might be."

"Well, come on over and play again, give us a chance to get our money back."

"If you got the energy, that is," another man said. "I hear that Angela is a little spitfire."

"Of course you hear," one of the other men said, "your missis would cut it off if she caught you sampling that first hand."

They all laughed and Clint said good night. He walked over to the bar to where Angela was standing, listening to a man who was doing all the talking.

Clint moved in right behind her and said to the bartender, "A beer."

"Comin' up."

Angela heard his voice and turned away from the other man while he was still talking.

"Hey, bitch!" the man said, grabbing her shoulder. "I'm talking to you."

"Take it easy, friend," Clint said to the man. "The lady and I have a previous engagement."

"Previous, hell," the man said. "I was talkin' to her, and she's goin' with me."

"Please—" Angela said to the man.

"Shut up, bitch!" the man said. "You're comin' upstairs with me."

"That ain't the way to talk to a lady—" the bartender started to say as he set Clint's beer down.

Angela was in his way and he didn't see the man go for his gun. Suddenly, the man was pointing his gun at the bartender.

"You gonna stop me, bartender?"

The bartender eyed the gun nervously and said, "Take it easy—"

Clint took hold of Angela's arm and moved her out from between him and the gunman.

"Look, friend," he said, "there are other girls here. One ain't worth getting killed over."

The man laughed, still pointing the gun at the bartender.

"I got the gun out, Mister," he said. "I ain't the one gonna get killed."

"Yes you are," Clint said. "If you don't put that gun away, I'll kill you."

The man eyed Clint and said, "You're bluffin'."

"By the time you take that gun off the bartender and point it at me, you'll be dead. That's a fact."

Now it was the gunman's turn to look nervous.

He was a little drunk and had gotten himself into a situation he probably would have liked to back away from, but if he did he'd look bad. Clint hoped that someone had gone for the sheriff, and he could keep the man talking until the lawman arrived.

"Now, all this over a woman?" Clint asked. "Hell, man, I'll buy you a drink and we'll forget the whole thing. Just put the gun away."

"Sh—she was talkin' to me," the man said, as if trying to claim that it wasn't his fault.

"Just passing the time while waiting for me, friend," Clint said. "Think back. Did she ever mention going upstairs?"

The man thought back and said, "Well, no—"

"See? Now put the gun away and let's have that drink. Bartender, get this gentleman whatever he wants, on me."

Nervously, the bartender's eyes were flicking from the gun to Clint and back to the gun.

"Go ahead," Clint told him.

"W—what'll you have?" the bartender asked the gunman.

The man was still trying to make up his mind what to do.

"Beer all right?" Clint asked. "I think you've had enough whiskey."

The man thought some more and then said, "Sure, beer's fine."

"Get my friend a beer," Clint told the bartender, "and make it a cold one."

The bartender drew a cold beer and set it in front of the gunman, moving cautiously, his eyes never leaving the gun, which was no longer pointed *at* him so much as in his general direction.

"Gotta put that gun away to drink it," Clint said to the man.

The gunman looked at Clint, then at the beer. He licked his lips, holstered the gun slowly, and then picked up the beer.

"There you go," Clint said, and at that moment the sheriff walked in.

"Got a problem here, Will?" the lawman asked the bartender.

The bartender looked at Clint, who shook his head slightly.

"Uh, no, Sheriff, it's all taken care of," the barkeep replied.

"Drink hearty, friend," Clint said. He turned, found Angela standing behind him and said, "Well, I'm ready. Let's go."

Hell, he thought, why not?

As he followed her to the stairs he heard the sheriff say to the gunman, "Hell, man, you sure got lucky. You know who that was . . ."

Chapter Six

Angela led Clint to a small room with a bed and a dresser. It didn't look like a room anyone lived in, and he guessed it wasn't.

Inside the room he reached for her but she scooted away from him.

"What's wrong?" he asked. "Not so eager now?"

"I have something for you," she said.

"I got that feeling downstairs," he said. "Why so eager down there, and so shy up here?"

She averted her eyes and said, "I ... don't like this kind of work."

"Can't say I blame you," he said. Suddenly, he didn't think he was up here for the reason he'd origi- nally thought. "What is it, Angela?"

"There was a man here, about a week or so ago," she said, nervously.

"A man?"

"From the government."

Suddenly he was all ears.

"He told you he was from the government?"

She nodded, hugging her bare arms as if she was cold.

"What else did he tell you?"

"He told me he'd get me out of here," she said. "He said somebody would be coming after him, if something happened to him. H—has something happened to him?"

"I don't know," Clint said. "He's disappeared, I know that much."

"And you're looking for him?"

"That's right."

"Are you . . . with the government, too?"

"Not exactly," he said. "He and I are friends, and I'd like to find out for sure if anything's happened to him."

"He promised to help me get away if I helped him," she said. "Will you keep his promise?"

"Yes, Angela," he said, "I'll help you. I'll keep his promise."

She reached into the waist of her skirt and came out with a small envelope.

"I didn't dare leave it lying around," she said, handing it to him.

"You did the right thing," he said, accepting it.

He turned away from her and opened the envelope. Inside was a note from West. Clint recognized his friend's handwriting. The note wasn't addressed to anyone in particular.

"Sheriff involved. Am heading northwest, towards Midnight. Take care of girl."

That was it, the whole message. It didn't tell Clint anything he might not have figured out on his own, except that West did head northwest. What remained now was for Clint to decide whether to follow him, head northeast, or confront the sheriff.

He turned back to Angela, who watched him closely with her huge, made-up eyes.

"Did you see a woman—"

"He asked me the same question," she said, cutting him off. "I didn't see no woman from the government, but then she wouldn't have come in here."

That was true.

Maybe she'd have gone to see the sheriff, though. Maybe the thing for Clint to do was to make like he was looking for Kate O'Hara. If he didn't mention West to the sheriff, maybe it would confuse the man. Clint could say he was looking for his sister—or his lover—and make no mention of West. If he was government, maybe the sheriff would expect him to ask about both of them.

"Does that help?" Angela asked.

"Yes, Angela," he said, tucking the note back into the envelope and then putting it in his shirt pocket, "it helps a lot."

"The other man, he was nice. He didn't try to . . . to make me go to bed with him."

"That's my friend," Clint said. "A decent man."

She smiled shyly now and said, "Him I wouldn't have minded going to bed with. He wouldn't have been like some of these men, the farmers and ranch hands who just want to . . . to use you, you know? For their own pleasure?"

"I know . . ." he said, lamely.

"You look like a decent man."

"I'd like to think so."

"If I go downstairs," she said, "I'll have to come up here with one of them."

"Angela—"

"We don't have to do anything," she said. "Maybe just sit and . . . talk."

As it turned out, they didn't have a lot to talk

about. She'd been born in a small town, and had worked in several small towns since then.

"I'm a whore," she said, "and I don't know nothing about sex. I just lie here and open my legs, you know?"

They were sitting on the bed and she moved closer to him.

"Angela—"

"Maybe you could show me something . . ."

"Angela, listen—"

"I mean, I ain't never been with a man who didn't think of anything but his own pleasure. There are other kinds of men, aren't there?"

The look on her face was so hopeful that he put his arm around her and said, "Yes, Angela, there are other kinds of men."

She leaned her head against his chest and stayed that way for a while.

The way she was leaning, with his arm around her, her right breast just naturally found its way into his hand, like somebody put it there. He could feel its weight and warmth through the fabric of her blouse.

If he went downstairs too soon the sheriff might get suspicious about what he and Angela had done up here.

He moved his hand slightly, so that he could slide it beneath the blouse and cup her naked breast. Her nipple hardened and he took hold of it with his fingers and rolled it a bit.

"Mmm," she said, her voice muffled by his chest, "that feels nice . . ."

He continued to manipulate her breasts, first one and then the other, and then she sat up and abruptly pulled the blouse over her head. Her breasts were small, but they were firm and round. Her nipples were dark brown, and distended.

He leaned over and took a nipple in his mouth, rolled it between his teeth and sucked it.

"Mmmm, oh," she said, "I ain't never had a man . . . do that. Mostly they just . . . just bite . . ."

He kissed her breasts, running his lips and tongue over the smooth flesh and she moaned and sighed.

He set her down on the bed and removed her skirt. When she was naked he hung his gunbelt on the bedpost and then removed his own clothes.

"Oh," she said, when she saw his swollen penis, "it's. . . . it's beautiful."

"Surely you've seen one before," he said.

"Most of them are so fast they just poke it in and get it over with," she said. "I never get a chance to see . . . oh!"

She stopped when he put his hand on her belly, rubbing it gently, and then slid his hand down to the black tangle of hair between her legs. His fingers found her, made her moist and wet, then delved into her. She bit her lip and lifted her hips to his hand. When he touched her swollen clit she gasped and came, her eyes wide.

"God," she said, "I ain't *never* felt nothing like that!"

A whore for how long, he wondered, and she'd never had an orgasm. All she'd been was a receptacle for some man's lust . . .

He moved down and gently ran his tongue over her wet puss. She moaned and grabbed two handfuls of the sheet beneath her.

"Lord, what are you doin'—"

She stopped short when his tongue moved into her, moving, lapping, and then along the length of her slit until he found her clit.

"Ooh, Jesus . . ." she cried as his tongue flicked at her, and then he closed his lips over her and sucked until she was writhing and bouncing beneath him.

Before the spasms could fade he mounted her and slowly entered her. She made a sound deep in her throat and wrapped her legs around him. Her nails scraped at his back as he drove into her, bringing her to yet another orgasm and then he finally allowed himself to explode inside of her . . .

Chapter Seven

Downstairs the sheriff coaxed the gunman out of the saloon and back to the ranch where he worked, and then moved to the end of the bar. After a few moments the bartender joined him.

"What happened, Will?" he asked.

"The cowboy started trouble over Angela, Sheriff. That feller—"

"Clint Adams."

"Yeah, Adams, he handled it without ever drawing his gun. You sure he's the Gunsmith?"

"He is."

"They why didn't he just kill the cowboy? He coulda gunned him easy."

"I don't know. What bothers me more is what he's doing here."

"You don't think he knows—"

"I don't think he knows anything," the sheriff said, "and I don't want him finding out anything, either. Wasn't it Angela who went upstairs with that government man?"

"Yeah, why? She don't know nothing."

"Maybe it's a coincidence," the sheriff said, rubbing his jaw. "Who approached who?"

"Whataya mean?"

"Did she go after him, or did he go after her?"

"I don't know," the bartender said. "He called her

over for a beer and they started talking."

"Keep an eye on her, Will," the sheriff said. "If she don't know nothing, let's keep it that way."

"Sure, Sheriff," the bartender said. "What are you gonna do about him?"

"I don't know, yet," the sheriff said, biting his bottom lip, "I just don't know."

Later, when they were both dressed, she said, "I don't know how to thank you, Mister."

"You don't have to."

"But ain't nobody ever given *me* pleasure before. I mean . . . was it okay for you?"

"You were wonderful, Angela," he said. "You don't belong here. After I find my friend we'll come back and get you out of here."

"Oh, promise?" she said, grabbing his hand like a kid who's just been promised candy.

"I promise," he said, squeezing her hand. "We'd better get downstairs now."

"All right."

"Wait," he said, and handed her some money.

"Unh-un," she said, "I said you wouldn't have to—"

"You'll have to show some money or your boss will be suspicious," he said.

"Oh . . . all right," she said, obviously uncomfortable about taking the money.

"Now let's go."

Walking down the steps behind Angela Clint could see that the sheriff was still there. He wondered if the man had timed him.

Angela went to one end of the bar and Clint went to the other, where the sheriff was.

"Buy you a drink, Sheriff," he asked, "or do you have one coming?"

"Sure," the lawman said, "I'll have a beer, Will."

"Make it two," Clint told the bartender.

"How was she?" the sheriff asked.

"A gentleman never tells, Sheriff."

The bartender brought the two beers and Clint drank half of his. Angela was young, and during their second frolic she'd been very eager. He was surprised at how tired he felt.

"Will—that's the bartender—was real impressed with the way you handled that cowboy," the sheriff said.

"He was just a little drunk," Clint said.

"That why you didn't kill him?"

"I didn't have any reason to kill him," Clint said. "He didn't really want to shoot anyone, anyway."

"Your experience tell you that?"

"Yes."

"You didn't exactly live up to your reputation, you know."

"I'm sorry about that, Sheriff," Clint said. "Next time I'll kill him, and maybe wound a few by-standers as well. Would that fit your picture of me?"

"Not my picture, Adams," the sheriff said. "You must have done something to earn that rep of yours."

"My curse," Clint said.

The sheriff frowned and put his half-finished beer on the bar.

"Be leavin' come morning?" he asked Clint.

"Maybe."

"What's there to keep you?"

"I'm looking for a woman."

"A woman? Didn't you just—"

"Another woman."

"So soon after—"

"A different woman," Clint said, "for a different reason."

"What woman? For what reason?"

"Her name's Kate O'Hara. Ever hear of her?"

"Can't say I have."

"Pretty woman, Irish," Clint said. "You'd remember. Red hair, some freckles—"

"Doesn't ring a bell. What's your interest in her?"

"She's my . . . fiancée."

"Fiance?" the sheriff said, not pronouncing the "e" at the end. "Does she know you like saloon girls?"

"She's got her own damned job," Clint said.

"Oh, what's that?"

"Damned if I know. Something secret, I think. She never would tell me."

"You're gettin' married and she won't tell you what she does for a living?"

"That's about the size of it."

"What makes you think she passed through here?"

"She sent me a telegraph message a while back, said she'd be heading this way."

"And you're trying to catch up to her?"

"Yep."

"What for?"

"Put my foot down," Clint said. "Either she stops this secret nonsense, or the wedding's off."

The sheriff was staring at Clint, who didn't like the story himself, so how could he expect the lawman to believe it. He waited as patiently as he could for the man to call him a liar. Jim West would have come up with a more plausible story, which only served to indicate what an amateur he was. Then again, West was missing, too, so maybe he *hadn't* come up with a more plausible story.

Clint reminded himself to ask West the next time he saw him.

"I could ask around tomorrow, if you like," the sheriff finally said. "Maybe find something out."

"I'd appreciate it."

"And if I don't find out anything?"

"I'll be leaving the next morning," Clint said. "Wouldn't be any reason for me to stay, then."

The sheriff nodded, apparently satisfied with that answer.

"What'd you say her name was?"

"O'Hara, Kate O'Hara."

The sheriff pushed away from the bar and said, "Be around tomorrow, I'll see what I can find out."

"Appreciate it, Sheriff."

The sheriff nodded and left, leaving his beer half finished.

When the bartender came over to retrieve the mug Clint asked, "Does he ever finish a beer?"

The bartender shrugged and moved away.

Clint turned, found Angela, exchanged a brief glance with her, and then left the saloon.

Chapter Eight

Clint finally decided that there was no way that the sheriff could believe that dumb story, so he went to his hotel room and prepared to sit up awake all night.

It didn't take all night.

First he became aware that someone was outside his door. He could hear the floorboards creaking.

Next, he saw that someone was outside his window. He could see the shadow moving.

He dropped off the bed to the floor and, gun in hand, waited.

Apparently, the two men had set this up carefully, because they both moved at the same time. The door was kicked open and the second man actually hurled himself through the window.

Clint shot the man coming through the door first, because the other man had landed on the floor and would need a few seconds to right himself.

He heard the first man grunt as his bullet hit him, and then he turned his attention to the second man, who had been faster than he'd expected. He was up on his knees already, but his eyes were not used to the darkness in the room, which was more dense than the darkness outside.

Clint had no such problem, and shot him once.

Then he moved to the lamp on the wall, hoping

that one of the men would still be alive to question.

No such luck.

Both of his shots had landed relatively close to the heart, close enough to cause death either instantaneously, or only moments later.

"Shit," he said.

He slammed the door and it remained ajar, damaged by the kick that had opened it. He heard the commotion outside as people began to fill the hall. He decided to take the window himself and get out of there before somebody got brave enough to come into the room.

He wanted to find the sheriff before the man found him.

Sheriff Wade Nichols heard the shots from his office and assumed that his objective had been achieved. He'd sent the two men to the hotel with strict instructions to make sure Clint Adams didn't survive the night.

He rose from behind his desk and slowly put his gun belt on. He'd have to make a show of responding to the noise to investigate the incident. Unfortunately, Clint Adams will have been killed by two men who had apparently broken into his room to rob him.

Shocking.

As he opened his office door and stepped outside, something round and cold pressed against his right temple before he could close the door.

"Step back inside," a voice said.

Clint Adams' voice.

"Shit," Sheriff Wade Nichols said.

"My sentiments exactly," Clint Adams said.

Chapter Nine

As they stepped into the office Clint relieved the sheriff of his gun and closed the door.

"Get the drapes, Sheriff," he instructed.

The sheriff pulled the drapes obediently. Clint was sure some nice town mother must have made them for him.

"Over by your desk."

The sheriff walked to the desk and started to sit.

"Wait."

He stopped.

Clint checked the drawers and found another gun in one of them. He removed it.

"Now sit."

Nichols sat.

"If I don't show up at the hotel to investigate the shots, somebody's going to come looking for me here."

"That's fine," Clint said, "and you'll just tell them you'll be right there."

"And if I don't?"

"I'll kill you."

"You wouldn't," the sheriff said, smugly.

"You just have to be brave enough to want to find out," Clint said.

Nichols' face fell.

"You want to deny you sent those two men to the hotel to kill me?"

"I ain't sayin' nothing," Nichols said.

Clint leaned forward and rapped the sheriff on the bridge of the nose with his gun.

"Ow, Jesus," the man said, his eyes immediately leaking tears as he grabbed his nose.

"All I have to do is hit you a little harder there and I'll break your nose," Clint said. "After that we can go to something else. Some fingers, maybe."

"What the hell do you want?"

"Kate O'Hara and Jim West."

"Who are they?" Nichols asked, lowering his hand.

Clint hit him in the same place, a little harder.

"Christ!" the sheriff said, raising his hands to ward off another blow.

"Your nose is stronger than I thought," Clint said. "I'm really going to have to rap it hard to break—"

"No, wait!"

"For what?"

"I gotta think."

"About what? A good lie?"

"West, is that the government man?"

Clint grinned.

"Now you've got it?"

"And O'Hara, that's the woman who came before him?"

"Right. My guess is she asked you straight out about some folks who were missing."

"I told her I didn't know nothing about that."

"But you were lying."

"Why should I lie?"

Nichols had one hand on his nose and the other flat on the desk. Clint brought the butt of his gun down on the man's little finger.

"Damn!" the sheriff cried out. He lowered his other hand from his face to grab the injured one and Clint hit him on the nose again. His nose was red and swollen by now, but still not broken.

"Stop, stop!" Nichols yelled. His eyes were tearing and he didn't know whether to hold his hand or his nose.

"Don't lie to me, Sheriff," Clint said. "You know something about the people who have been disappearing, don't you?"

"I can't—" Nichols said. "They'll kill me."

"I'll kill you first."

"You can't—" Nichols said. "You can't kill me. You need me."

"To do what? If you're not going to talk to me, why do I need you alive?"

"I can help you—"

"But will you?"

"You can't do this," Nichols said. "I'm the sheriff. I'm the law—"

Clint leaned forward and Nichols flinched, thinking he was going to be hit again. Instead, Clint plucked the badge from his shirt and dropped it to the desk top.

"You just resigned your office."

Before someone could come looking for Nichols Clint marched the man out through the back door, and over to the livery stable.

"Saddle my horse," he instructed him, "and then yours."

"Where are you taking me?" Nichols demanded.

"We're going for a ride, into the triangle."

"Into the what?"

"Never mind," Clint said. "I'm taking you with me to find O'Hara and West and the other nineteen people who disappeared."

"I can't help you—" the sheriff said, turning away from the mustang.

"Keep saddling the horse," Clint said. "In your office you said you *could* help me, now you say you can't. Which is it?"

"Look, I don't know anything—"

"Sure you do."

"I don't know where anything *is*!"

"We'll see."

"I can't take you anywhere!"

Nichols' tone was becoming more and more strident. The more he said he couldn't do something, the more convinced Clint became that he could.

"Then I'll leave your body for the buzzards," Clint said. "I don't take it very kindly when people try to kill me, Sheriff. Was it your idea, or did someone tell you to have it done?"

"I—it wasn't my idea!"

"You protest too strongly, Sheriff," Clint said. "That's good, now saddle yours."

"It's dark out—"

"We'll manage."

"One of the horses could break his leg—"

"If that happens you'll walk and I'll ride."

"Adams, this is crazy," Nichols said. "You don't know what you're dealing with, here!"

"Why don't you tell me, then?"

"I can't!"

"Then saddle that horse and let's get moving," Clint said. "Before anything can happen to me, Nichols, it's going to happen to you, first. I promise you that."

Chapter Ten

"This was stupid," Wade Nichols said.

Clint didn't respond.

"You brought us out here with no supplies, and no water," Nichols complained.

"I have water," Clint said.

"Sure, *you* have water," Nichols said, "but you won't give me any."

"You know what you have to do for it, Nichols."

"Sheriff Nichols, to you."

"Nope," Clint said, "ex-Sheriff Nichols."

Clint had stopped thinking about Nichols as a sheriff. He had respect for the law and it helped to do what he had to do if he didn't think of Nichols as a sheriff. The man didn't deserve to wear a badge, anyway.

"I'm a sheriff, duly elected—"

"And what do you think the townspeople would say if I told them that their sheriff had set me up to be killed?" Clint asked.

"They'd never believe you," Nichols said. "That's why you ran."

"I ran because I don't have the time to waste trying to convince them," Clint said. "When this is all over I'll go back and straighten everything else."

"When this is over," Nichols said, "you'll be a dead man, Adams."

"You're getting pretty brave for a thirsty man, Nichols."

They had camped and made a fire after Clint had taken Nichols from town. Clint had made a show of making some coffee and eating some beef jerky, and never even offered Nichols any.

Now it was mid-afternoon and the sheriff's lips were starting to dry and crack. To make his point stronger Clint took a sip from the diminishing amount of water that was still in his canteen.

"Adams, you don't know what you're dealing with here—"

"That's all I've been hearing from you, Nichols," Clint said. "I'm waiting for you to tell me what I *am* dealing with."

"I can't—damn it, man, can't you see that?"

"No, I can't," Clint said.

He could see that the man was frightened of something—or of someone. More frightened than he was of the immediate danger posed by Clint Adams.

What could scare a man that much?

"Look, Nichols," Clint said, trying a different tact, "all I'm doing is looking for two of my friends who have disappeared."

"Your friends?"

"Right."

"The woman and the government man?"

"That's right."

"That's as lame as the other story you told me, Adams," Nichols said. "Chances are the woman was a government agent, too, and so are you."

"That's how you figure it."

"That's the only way I *can* figure it."

"Well, you think about it for a while," Clint said. "We'll camp soon for lunch."

"Lunch?"

"Yeah," Clint said, "I think I've still got some beef jerky left. What's the next town?"

Nichols didn't answer, but Clint was just making conversation. He knew that the next town was called Benson, and he planned to stock up on supplies there. What he hadn't decided was what to do with Nichols. If he took him into town he'd start squawking about being the sheriff of Mesa, and Clint would have to take the time to explain the situation to the local law.

No, his best bet was to truss Nichols up and leave him somewhere while he went into town and got outfitted.

Maybe they'd come to a water hole between now and then.

Kate O'Hara was worried.

She'd ceased being afraid, because she'd been afraid so long that she had started to ignore the fear. Now she was simply worried, about herself, and about whoever Cartwright would send looking for her. Then there was also all of the other people who had disappeared for her to worry about, the people she had been sent here to find.

Were they being held, as she was?

She was blindfolded and tied to a chair, and she had never seen the room that she was being held in. The only thing she knew was what her nose and ears told her.

The room was damp, her nose told her that. She

could smell the water, and even feel the dampness on her sweaty body.

Her ears told her that whoever it was who was bringing her food three times a day and feeding her was descending a flight of steps before they got to the door of the room. She also believed—and this was her nose, telling her this—that whoever was feeding her had been a man each time. She couldn't tell if it was the same man, but she felt sure that it had been a man each time.

She was thankful for meals, because not only did they allow her to keep her strength up, but they helped her tick off the days. By her reckoning she'd been here over two weeks, almost seventeen days.

Why had she been kept here so long? Why had she been kept alive all this time if she was a danger to someone?

The last thing she remembered was making camp one night. She couldn't believe that anyone had managed to get so close to her without her hearing it, but before she knew what was happening a hood had been thrown over her head, and she hadn't seen daylight since.

She was worried, all right.

Would she ever see daylight again?

In a nearby room a man lay on a pallet bed, unconscious. He had been unconscious or semiconscious since his arrival at this place, roused only long enough to be fed, and then put to sleep by some drug that was injected into his arm.

He was blindfolded, even when asleep, and around his wrist was a handcuff, the twin of which was hooked through a metal ring that was imbedded in a stone wall.

The captors of Kate O'Hara and Jim West felt justified in assuming that the man was a larger threat than the woman. For this reason he was manacled and kept drugged, while she was simply tied to a chair and fed three times a day. Once in a while she would even be allowed to stretch her arms and legs, just to keep the circulation going.

On occasion, the men who were caring for these two wondered why they were being kept alive, but those occasions were few and far between. They were hired help, and had no idea what was behind the decision to keep them alive.

That decision was being made by one man, and none of the "help" had ever even seen him.

Chapter Eleven

"You can't leave me here like this," Nichols complained.

Clint tested the ropes that were holding Nichols' arms and legs and then stood up.

"Nichols, you're always trying to tell me what I can and can't do. Why don't you try telling me something else for a change?"

"I can't—"

"I know," Clint said in disgust, "I've heard that before."

He turned and walked to Nichols' horse, and secured the reins to a low hanging branch of the tree he'd just tied Nichols to. Content that neither man nor horse could get free on their own, he walked to his own horse.

"I'll be back before nightfall, Nichols."

"You bastard!" Nichols shouted. "What if a bobcat or cougar comes by?"

"Talk real nice to them and they'll leave you alone," Clint said, mounting up.

"If I get loose, Adams—"

"If you get loose, Nichols, you won't have a gun. You'd be safer just waiting here for me."

Clint knew he was taking a chance leaving the man's horse behind, but he didn't want to ride into town leading it. That could cause too many questions to be asked.

If Nichols did somehow manage to get loose he'd be able to ride to the nearest town for help. Still, even if he lost him, having Nichols had done him no good up to now. He was starting to think the man would never talk. So far threats hadn't worked. He wondered how hungry and thirsty the man would have to get before he would talk.

Reasonably sure that the only way Nichols could get away was for someone to help him, Clint felt sure the man would still be there when he returned. He had chosen this stand of sycamore because, from a distance, Nichols was out of sight. Someone would actually have to ride up to these trees to see him— and then, of course, they'd have to believe whatever story he told.

"If you're still here when I get back, Nichols," Clint said, "I might just feed you."

"Adams!" Nichols shouted. "Don't leave me here, Adams!"

Clint waved and rode off toward the town of Benson.

Benson was a small town, a stopping off place like he knew the town of Midnight would be. Still, it had a general store, and the supplies that he needed. What it didn't have was a telegraph office, so he wouldn't be able to send a message to Cartwright in Washington.

Clint smiled at the prospect of William Masters Cartwright having kittens wondering what the hell had happened to him? Then the smile fell away. If he didn't contact the man soon he might try to find some other chump to send into Mesa, looking for Kate, West *and* Clint.

Clint wanted the string of missing agents to stop with him. Sometime within the next twenty-four hours he was going to have to find a telegraph line.

He rode up to the general store and dismounted.

William Masters Cartwright looked up as Gloria Manners entered his office.

"Anything?" he asked.

"Nothing, sir."

Cartwright slammed his palm down on the top of his desk in anger.

"He never even notified us that he had arrived safely in Mesa."

"He may not have been able to, sir," she said. "Who knows who's monitoring the telegraph line?"

Rubbing his jaw Cartwright said, "You do have a point, Gloria. Still, if I don't hear from him in a day or so, I'll have to take drastic measures."

"Sir?"

"I'll have to have the army sent in, maybe even declare the area under martial law."

"Can you do that, sir?"

Looking uncomfortable Cartwright said, "Well, no, *I* can't do it, but I can suggest that it be done. Something has to be done!"

"Yes, sir."

"If I do that, though," he went on, "and those missing people are still alive, I might be causing their death."

"It's a difficult decision, sir."

Cartwright looked at her and then said, "What would you do, Miss Manners?"

"Me, sir?"

"Yes. Come on, you must have an opinion."

"Well..." Gloria said, thinking rapidly, "yes, I do..."

"Well then? What is it?"

"I'd give Clint Adams forty-eight hours, sir, instead of twenty-four."

He stared at her and then said softly, "Yes, you would, wouldn't you. You have a lot of faith in his ability, don't you?"

"Jim West always has, sir," she said, "and he has come through in the past, every time."

"Yes, he has," Cartwright said, "every time. That's what worries me."

"What's that, sir?"

He looked at her and said, "A man can only keep up a perfect record for so long."

Gloria frowned and said, "Yes, sir."

Clint bought only as much as he would be able to comfortably carry. When he reached Nichols he could separate things into two loads, so that each horse could carry an equal amount. He bought coffee, dried beef, bacon, flour and some canned goods.

As an after thought he asked the clerk, "Do you sell whiskey?"

"Sure do."

"One bottle."

"Right, sir."

He paid for the supplies and carried them out to his horse in a canvas sack. When he reached the animal he saw a man standing next to it, inspecting it.

"Problem?" he asked.

The man straightened up and turned to face him,

and he saw the badge. The man wearing it had to be close to sixty, with a lined, leathery face and white hair showing beneath his hat.

"I was about to ask you the same thing," the sheriff said. "Horse looks like he's been rid a ways."

"He has," Clint said. "Now that I've got my supplies he'll get some rest soon."

"Headin' anywheres in particular?"

"Nope," Clint said, "and not going anywhere in particular."

"Just goin', huh?"

"That's right."

Clint tied the sack to his saddle and mounted up.

"Yep," the lawman said, "I remember being that young, once."

"Maybe you can help me out, Sheriff."

"Be happy to, young feller."

"Where's the nearest telegraph line?"

"Well . . . you'd have to ride a ways to get to it. Place called Chance Awakening."

"That's a strange name for a town."

"T'aint a town, really. More like a settlement. Used to be a fort some years past, which is why they got a line there."

"Where is this place?"

"Have to ride east about forty miles to get to it."

Forty miles east, Clint thought. Right into the center of the "triangle."

"None up the line, in another town?"

"Not along here," the sheriff said. "All the towns along here are like this one."

"I see. Well, thanks, Sheriff."

"Got an urgent message to send?"

"Not urgent," Clint said. "Just an uncle who likes

to know I'm all right from time to time."

"Well, you let him know, hear?"

"I will, Sheriff." Clint said. "Thanks."

When Clint returned to the spot where he'd left former Sheriff Wade Nichols it was getting dark. The man was still there, lashed to the tree.

"All right, Nichols," Clint said, dismounting, "dinner'll be served in no time, as soon as I start a fire. Yeah, that's right, I've decided to feed you, just so you won't die on me until I'm finished with you."

Clint stopped talking and thought that Nichols was being pretty quiet for a man who had to be mightily pissed off.

"Nichols, you asleep?"

He approached the man and had almost reached him when he saw what was wrong. In the shadows of the trees he hadn't noticed it before, but Nichols' chest was covered with blood.

"Jesus," Clint said, and bent to examine the man. Nichols' head was resting on his chest, and as he lifted it he saw that his throat had been neatly cut. The blood had covered his chest and soaked into his clothes.

He was about as dead as a man could get.

Chapter Twelve

Clint unsaddled and released Nichols' horse, and then put some distance between himself and the body tied to the tree.

He camped, built a fire and made some coffee. He had no appetite for food.

Over coffee, he thought about how he had gotten Wade Nichols—*Sheriff* Wade Nichols—killed. There was no denying the fact that it was his fault the man was dead, but should he be feeling guilty about it? Hell, the man had tried to have *him* killed just the night before, hadn't he?

Putting aside for a moment the moral questions that Nichols' death had raised Clint thought about another question.

Who had killed him?

The body had not been relieved of its valuables, and the horse was still there, so he hadn't been robbed. That left only one possibility.

The very people he was afraid of had found him there and killed him.

Another victim of the Arizona Triangle?

Had they been following the two of them the whole time? That thought sent a chill down Clint's back, because if someone *had* been following them since they left Mesa, his instincts had let him down, because he hadn't sensed a thing.

He preferred to think that they had found Nichols —somehow—and just considered the move prudent to kill him, rather than just release him.

Why?

As a warning to Clint?

Why warn him?

Why not just wait and kill him, too?

Did they think that he was a government agent? Had that kept them from killing him? And if so, did that mean that Kate O'Hara and Jim West were still alive?

And if they *were* still alive, then why wasn't Clint in the same place they were?

Too many questions rolling around inside his head. All he wanted to do was sleep, and he couldn't do that.

Or could he?

He woke the next morning with a feeling of mild surprise.

He had decided the night before that he needed sleep more than he needed to keep watch. Hell, if the people who killed Nichols had wanted him they could have had him easy enough. Maybe he was being watched. Maybe they wanted to see which way he was going to jump come morning.

And maybe they had watched him sleep.

If they were there—somewhere—watching him, they had let him sleep, and for this he was grateful.

No longer concerned with trying to stay out of sight he made himself a breakfast of bacon and biscuits cooked in the bacon grease, and downed a pot of strong coffee. Thus fortified he cleaned his utensils and put them away, then saddled his horse and mounted up.

He headed east, for the settlement with the odd name of Chance Awakening.

Chapter Thirteen

Chance Awakening had been born only five years before.

Derek Vincannon had come to Arizona from the east to try and find a new home for himself and his family. Along the way his wife, his two daughters and his son were joined by other families they met, until—when they reached the deserted Fort Myerson —they were virtually a wagon train of six wagons and thirty-three people.

Now, five years after Vincannon and the others had founded the settlement of Chance Awakening, their population was a controlled 112.

The grounds inside the fort had been turned into homes, and behind the fort were the stores and shops. The people felt safer with their homes behind the high walls of the fort.

When Clint Adams came to the front gate of the fort he saw the sign stating: THE SETTLEMENT OF *CHANCE AWAKENING.* VISITORS WELCOME.

He was about to cry out a hello when the gates started to open. He waited patiently and was finally rewarded when a man holding a rifle stepped out.

"Hello," the man greeted.

"That's a funny way to greet welcome visitors," Clint said, "with a rifle in your hands."

"Just a precaution," the man said, squinting up at

Clint. "Is that what you're planning to do, visit?"

"A stopover is more like it," Clint said. "I understand you have a telegraph key here."

"We do."

"I'd like to use it."

"Step down and bring your horse in," the man said. "You'll have to talk to Derek."

"Derek?"

"Derek Vincannon," the man said. "He's our—well, our mayor, for want of a better word. Step down and come on in, friend. If you're hungry, we can take care of that, too."

Clint dismounted and followed the man inside, leading his horse behind him.

Inside he was surprised by what he saw. Probably the only thing that remained from the fort's active days was the flagpole in the center of the grounds. The buildings—the barracks, the stockade, the officer's quarters and such—had all been turned into homes, complete with white picket fences.

"Give your horse to Jeremy, there," the man said, indicating another man standing nearby, also holding a rifle.

Clint gave the reins to the second man and the first one said, "Come with me."

"Would it be all right if I was to know your name?" Clint asked.

"Tally," the man said, "Vincent Tally. This way, please."

"Adams," Clint said.

"What?"

"My name is Clint Adams."

"You can introduce yourself to Derek."

Clint followed Vincent Tally past all the homes to

a back gate, which led into a street lined with stores and shops. He looked for a saloon, or a hotel, or a sheriff's office, but saw none—but after all, this wasn't a town.

There were businesses being run, though: Feed & Grain, General Store, Café, Dress Shop, Gunsmith, Hardware Store, everything you'd find in a town, large or small.

"Derek's office is here," Tally said, pointing to a building.

Clint guessed that this must have been a hotel, once. As they approached it he thought he heard a chattering noise from another, smaller building.

They went inside, through the lobby and what must have once been a dining room. Now they were deserted, the old hotel desk clean, but not being used. The dining room still had tables and chairs, and they were all clean, as well.

At the back of the dining room Tally stopped at a door and knocked.

"Come in!" a voice called.

The man opened the door and allowed Clint to precede him.

At first glance Derek Vincannon was an impressive figure. As he stood Clint saw that he was easily six-four, or more, with wide shoulders and a narrow waist. His hair, eyebrows and full beard were slate gray, as were his piercing, slightly sunken eyes.

Around his waist he wore an old navy Colt in a holster worn too high. His clothes were simple, jeans, a clean work shirt, nothing elaborate, and yet he gave off an air of authority that was undeniable.

"Vincent," he said.

"This stranger came to the front gate, Derek. Says he's just stopping over."

Vincannon turned his intense gaze on Clint and said, "My name is Derek Vincannon. Welcome to Chance Awakening."

"Thank you," Clint said. "My name is Clint Adams."

"Mr. Adams, you'll excuse me if I satisfy myself of something?"

"Uh, sure," Clint said, unsure of what he was agreeing to.

"You are not on the run are you?"

"On the—no, I'm not on the run."

"Wanted by the law?"

"No."

"You are certain."

"That isn't the sort of thing I'd forget, Mr. Vincannon."

The man stared at him for a few moments, then his face broke into a smile that didn't touch his eyes.

"No, I don't suppose it is. Please, have a seat."

"Thank you."

"That's all, Vincent."

"Yes, Derek."

Tally withdrew and closed the door behind him.

"May I offer you something? We have no hard liquor here at the settlement, but we do brew our own beer."

"No, thank you."

"Well . . . perhaps at dinner, then?"

"Perhaps."

"You'll dine at my home, with my family and myself—if that is all right with you."

"Well, you don't have a hotel, but I did see a café—"

"Nonsense," Vincannon said. "You are a guest. We will not make you pay for your meal."

"You're very generous."

"I am an excellent judge of character, Mr. Adams," Vincannon said. "I asked you questions point blank and you answered them without hesitating, without flinching. I believe you."

"Maybe I'm just a good liar."

Vincannon laughed.

"I'm sure you are," he said, "but not in this instance."

"No," Clint said, "not in this instance."

"Where are you bound?"

"Nowhere in particular," Clint said.

"What brought you here? Surely, you did not know of our settlement . . ."

"Actually, I did," Clint said, sensing that he was still being tested, felt out.

"Oh?"

"The sheriff in Benson told me about it."

"Did he? And why would he do that?"

"I was looking for a telegraph key. He said the closest one was here."

Vincannon smiled at that, amused.

"Did I say something funny?"

"I'm sorry," Vincannon said. "I don't know the sheriff in Benson, but he was probably remembering a time when the telegraph key here was active."

"It no longer is?"

"I'm sorry," Vincannon said, "but even if it was, we do not have anyone here who could operate it."

Clint frowned. Approaching the fort he had seen

the telegraph lines still riding high on the poles. He regretted that he had never become very proficient in operating a key, and he was not even certain that he still knew how. Still, he would have liked to have a look at it.

"That's unfortunate."

"Was there someone in particular you wanted to contact?"

"My Uncle," Clint said, lying for the first time, and conscious of Vincannon's still intense eyes. "He worries when I'm not in contact."

"You are close to this uncle?"

"Very," Clint said. "He is the only living family I have left."

"That is unfortunate," Vincannon said, then hurriedly added, "not that you have an uncle, but that he is the only living family you have. I take it you never married?"

"No," Clint said.

"That's a shame, too," Vincannon said. "A man should have a family. I have a wife and three children."

"That's very nice."

"Of course," Vincannon said, looking down at the top of his desk, "they're not children anymore. My son is twenty-five, my two daughters are twenty and eighteen."

"I see."

Abruptly, Vincannon looked up at him again.

"Well, I *am* sorry that we cannot accommodate your need for a telegraph key," Vincannon said, "but if you'd consent to stay the night we can certainly feed you and give you a warm bed."

"I'd appreciate that," Clint said. The man's tone

was pleasant enough, but Clint couldn't help but feel that his good humor and generous nature were a contrivance. "I'm willing to pay—"

"Nonsense," Vincannon said, waving the offer away impatiently, "you are our guest. Please, come with me and I will show you where you will sleep, and where you can freshen up. Dinner should be ready shortly."

Vincannon rose and Clint did likewise.

"I will have to tell my wife that we're having a guest for dinner," Vincannon said as they walked through the hotel, "but she always makes more than enough. And, of course, you will have questions."

"Questions?"

"About the settlement."

"I'm not a nosy man, by nature—"

"Nonsense," Vincannon said, "we're proud of what we have here. If you don't let me explain it to you, I will bust."

"Very well," Clint said, uneasily, "I'll ask questions."

There was one question Clint wouldn't ask, and that was why Vincannon was lying to him.

He was sure that the chattering noise he'd heard as he approached the hotel with Tally *was* a telegraph key—and an active one!

Chapter Fourteen

Clint washed his face in the basin he'd been provided. The water was ice cold, as if it had come from a stream or a well.

He thought about his answers to Derek Vincannon's questions about being wanted by the law. Was he wanted, back in Mesa? Had anyone connected him with the disappearance of the sheriff? And when the sheriff's body was found and identified, would he be wanted for the murder of a law enforcement official? That was something William Masters Cartwright would have to help him out of, whether he wanted to or not.

Following Vincannon back through the "town" he had listened intently, but had not heard the chatter of the telegraph key again. Whoever had been operating it might have been told to stop while he was within earshot.

Walking through the "fort" he saw that some of the old buildings had been torn down to make room for the homes that had been built. One building that remained and had not been modified was the old guard house.

"I hope you won't mind staying here," Vincannon said. "We use it for visitors."

Visitors, Clint wondered to himself, or prisoners?

"I've stayed in worse places," Clint said.

"I'll have some water brought to you so you can clean up. You can see my house from here. It's that one, at the end of the row nearest the back wall."

And the largest of all the homes, Clint noticed, further from the home next to it than all the others. Derek Vincannon liked his privacy, and the larger house would be in keeping with his authority.

Clint dried his face now and walked into the jail cell in back of the guard house. He looked out the window and saw Vincent Tally, up on the wall over the gate, holding his rifle in his arms. There were other men at various positions on the wall, as well. Apparently the people of Chance Awakening needed to feel *very* safe.

His saddlebags had already been brought to the guard house before he got there, and he removed a fresh shirt and put it on. His sack of supplies was also there, along with his rifle. Just to satisfy himself he went through his own belongings and finally decided that someone had been through them, as well. He had some letters in there and he was sure that he'd tucked the flaps of the envelopes back in after reading them, and now the flaps were out.

It must have been the policy in Chance Awakening to familiarize themselves with strangers—without the stranger's knowledge. Well, that was okay, he thought, repacking his saddlebags. There was nothing damning in any of the letters. One was from Rick Hartman in Labyrinth, and the other two from women he knew. One was from Anne Archer, and he resisted reading it again. All of the letters were from friends, and none of them referred to him as "The Gunsmith." In fact, he never carried anything that referred to him by reputation.

He recalled that there were three women in the Vincannon household, so he took a little extra time until he was reasonably certain he was presentable, then left the guard house and strolled across the compound towards the Vincannon house.

What he really wanted to do was go into "town" and see if he couldn't find that telegraph key, but that was going to have to wait until after dark.

He knew he'd been lied to about the key, but more than wanting to know why, he wanted to get to that key.

As he crossed the compound he found his path blocked by Vincent Tally, who seemed to have timed it so that they would intersect.

"Mr. Tally," Clint said.

"Having dinner at Derek's house?" Tally asked. The look on his face was not a friendly one. He seemed to be making no effort to hide his displeasure at Clint's presence.

Tally was a man in his late twenties, and obviously was *not* in any authority. Maybe he simply resented the fact that a stranger was dining with his leader.

"I've been invited, yes."

"He has two daughters," Tally said.

"So he said."

"One is named Mara."

"I'll remember that."

"Remember it well," Tally said. "Mara is mine." With that Tally turned and walked away.

A jealous suitor, was that all Vincent Tally was? That remained to be seen.

Clint continued his walk to the Vincannon house. He opened the picket fence, stepped inside the yard, and closed the gate behind him. He looked around at the garden and was surprised that the soil here would be conducive to such a successful and well kept garden.

"My wife has a green thumb," Derek Vincannon said.

Clint looked up and saw that Vincannon was watching him from the doorway.

"It's very nice."

"Please," Vincannon said, "supper is about to be put on the table. Come in, come in . . ."

Clint approached the door and, as Vincannon stepped back to allow him to enter, he suddenly had a sense of foreboding, as if he shouldn't enter.

But he did.

Chapter Fifteen

Clint was pleasantly surprised at how the dinner went.

He was also pleasantly surprised at Vincannon's family, all of whom seemed to be very pleased to have a stranger to dinner.

His son was the Jeremy who had taken Clint's horse from him. He was also very likely the one who had gone through Clint's saddlebags, but at dinner the younger Vincannon man was pleasant, well spoken, and courteous.

Julie Vincannon, Derek's wife, was a lovely woman in her forties and a shock of gray running through her raven dark hair on the right side. The gray didn't seem to bother her, probably because she was secure in her loveliness, which time did not seem to be able to do anything to dim.

The two daughters, Mara and Melissa, were lucky to favor their mother.

Melissa, the eighteen year old, was the true beauty of the two. She had long, lustrous black hair like her mother, big dark eyes, a full, expressive mouth and a generously proportioned body. At eighteen she probably still had some ripening to do, which was a frightening thought. God, he thought, what would she look like when she reached full womanhood.

Although not as classically lovely as her mother

or her sister, Clint could see why Vincent Tally would be jealous of Mara Vincannon.

Her hair was lighter than her mother's and sister's, a brown that probably came from her father before his turned gray. She wore it pulled back behind her head, which showed off the fine bone structure of her face. She had large eyes, but they were hazel rather than dark. She had a full mouth, but it was sensuous rather than expressive. Of the three women, she was the more blatantly sexual, and Clint couldn't help but react to her gaze every time she turned it on him. She spoke the least of any of the family, but her eyes seemed to say the most.

Clint had the distinct feeling that she wanted to talk to him in private.

Of course, he got the same feeling from Melissa, the young one, but he *knew* why she wanted to get him alone. She was sitting the closest to him and had been using her feet on him since they had first sat down. She would run her bare foot up and down his leg, and try to fit her toes up his trouser leg. She talked the most, too, wanting to know where he had been and where he was going.

"Ooh, I'd just love to travel," she said at one point, which got her a clouded look from her father and a worried glance from her mother.

"Mother and Father are afraid I'll run off with the first attractive man I meet," Melissa said.

"Melissa," her mother said, and Clint saw Derek Vincannon's jaw tighten.

"I think it's only natural for them to worry about you, Melissa," Clint said.

"Thank you, Mr. Adams."

"Please call me Clint, Ma'am."

Melissa had been calling him Clint since their introduction.

"There's not much around here for a girl to do, you know," Melissa went on.

"There is enough work to keep you busy," her mother said.

"Oh, pooh," Melissa said, "I wasn't thinking about work, Mother." She looked at Clint and said, "I was talking about fun, I was talking about meeting interesting people . . . interesting men! The men here are so boring, even Mara has to settle for that deadly boring Vincent Tally."

"I have no desire to settle for anyone—" Mara began, but her father cut them both off curtly.

"Melissa—" her father said, warningly.

"Melissa, help me clear the table," her mother said.

"Yes, Mother." She seemed properly chastised by the only word her father had spoken at dinner.

"I'll help, too, Mother," Mara offered.

"No," her mother said, "you stay here with your father and brother and Mr.—I mean, Clint."

"Yes, Mother."

Mara looked at Clint and he knew that she was going to carry the conversation now. He finally knew what had been happening during dinner. The women —and Jeremy—had been carrying the conversation, letting Derek Vincannon listen to Clint's responses and study them.

"Will you be leaving in the morning, Clint?" she asked him.

"Yes," Clint said. "I'll want to find a telegraph key as soon as possible." He looked at Vincannon and asked, "You wouldn't happen to know where the nearest *working* key was, would you?"

"I'm sorry," Vincannon said, "no. We know very little of what happens or what exists outside the settlement."

"You never leave?" Clint asked.

"Oh, some of us do go to neighboring towns for supplies," he said, "but that is all. We have no desire to leave."

That wasn't the impression Clint had been getting from Melissa, and he even felt that Mara wanted to leave, too. She hadn't said as much, but he had seen the look in her eyes as her sister talked about it.

"Apple pie," Julie Vincannon said, as she and Melissa reentered the room.

"Momma makes the best apple pie in the settlement," Jeremy said.

Jeremy favored his father. He was not as tall, but he was still over six feet, with wide shoulders and narrow hips. While the girls had benefited from their mother's bone structure, Jeremy had his father's strong jaw line and chin.

Clint sampled the apple pie and found it delicious. In fact, the entire meal had been one of the finest he'd ever eaten, and he told Julie Vincannon as much.

"Thank you," she said. "Would you like some more coffee?"

"Yes, please."

"I'll get it, Momma," Melissa said, leaping up from her chair and going to the kitchen.

Melissa returned with the coffee pot and stood next to Clint to pour it for him. He felt her hip settle firmly against his arm, and wondered if anyone else was noticing. She had a fine, solid hip, and he could feel its warmth right through both of their clothes.

After the coffee Julie said, "All right, girls, time to do the dishes and leave the men to talk."

Dutifully, both girls got up and followed their mother to the kitchen, but Melissa turned and gave Clint a longing glance.

Clint had a feeling that the idle chitchat had been all used up.

Chapter Sixteen

"You haven't said much through dinner, Mr. Vincannon," Clint said, deciding to be frank. "Still trying to make up your mind about something?"

Vincannon stared at him for a few moments, then smiled one of those smiles that never made it to his eyes.

"You're observant," he said, "and you know when you're being observed."

"I just don't know why."

He looked at Jeremy, but the younger Vincannon now seemed content to let his father carry the conversation.

"We're very protective about what we have here, Mr. Adams," the elder Vincannon said.

"That's why the guards on the walls?"

"Yes, and we have lookouts posted."

That bothered Clint. He had not seen a lookout on his way in. That meant they were not amateurs, which made this whole situation even more perplexing.

"What is it you're trying to protect, Mr. Vincannon?"

He spread his big hands and said, "Why, our homes, Mr. Adams. Just our homes. When we first settled here we had some troubles with strangers. A group of them came here, supposedly as visitors."

"What happened?"

"They tried to rob us," he said. "They mistreated our women."

"And?"

"And we were fortunate enough to be able to fight them off," he said. "We do not ever want a repeat of that incident."

"It seems harsh to judge all strangers by that one bad experience—"

"By doing so we avoid another unpleasant incident," Vincannon said. "Surely you can see that."

"Sure," Clint said, "sure I can. So you're naturally suspicious of all strangers. That's fine, but the guards, and the lookouts—"

"That may all seem excessive to you, Mr. Adams, but to us, for our peace of mind, it is a necessity."

After a moment Clint said, "Well, of course the decision of how to live is yours."

"Are you curious about how we came to be here?" Vincannon asked.

"I'd be lying if I said no."

Vincannon told him the story of leaving the east to come west, of encountering other families who were also looking for homes.

"We traveled together, and when we found this place we decided to go no further."

"You seem to have made yourselves quite a home here," Clint said.

"Oh, we have, sir, we surely have."

"What about the army?"

"What about them?"

"What if they want their fort back?"

Clint saw Jeremy toss his father a sharp glance.

"This place was deserted when we came here," Vincannon said.

"That may be, but it must still be owned by the army," Clint said. "Don't tell me you never considered that? That they might want to activate it again, some day?"

Vincannon frowned.

"Frankly, no, it never did occur to me. I—we— simply assumed that since it was deserted . . ."

"I don't mean to alarm you," Clint said, "but perhaps you should contact the army and let them know what you've accomplished here. I'm sure they'd be . . . understanding . . ."

"Perhaps," Vincannon said, "perhaps that would be advisable."

"In fact," Clint said, "you could use that telegraph key."

"I thought I made it clear that the key was not working," Vincannon said.

"You admit you have no one who can work it," Clint said. "Perhaps it can be activated. If you'd let me take a look at it—"

"No," Derek Vincannon said, "it is not in working order, of that I am sure. Besides, I would not want to delay you. You'll want to get enough rest tonight, and an early start in the morning."

Clint didn't like being *told* what he wanted to do, but he did not protest.

"Maybe you're right," he said. "I noticed that there is no saloon in town—"

"We do not believe in having hard liquor, or . . . tawdry women at the settlement," Vincannon said. "You understand."

"Yes, of course," Clint said. "I suppose, then, that

there's nothing left for me to do but turn in."

"We generally retire early here," Vincannon said.

"I'm sure you do," Clint said, rising. Both Vincannon men rose with him. "Would you please say good night to your wife and daughters for me."

"Of course. I'll see you to the door."

The house was built on two levels, and downstairs there was a kitchen, a living room, an office, and the dining room in which they had just eaten.

Derek Vincannon walked Clint to the front door and opened it for him.

"If I do not see you in the morning, please, have a safe journey."

"Thank you."

"I will make sure that Jeremy is up early to get your horse ready for you."

"I appreciate it."

"Good night, Mr. Adams . . . and good-by."

"Good-by, Mr. Vincannon. Thank you for your hospitality."

Clint left the house and Vincannon wasted no time in closing the door behind him.

It was dark, but it was still early—much earlier than Clint had ever gone to bed in recent memory. Still, there was no way to pass the time, and he did not want to go looking for that telegraph key until very late, when he was sure that everyone was bedded down.

There was nothing for him to do but go back to his quarters—the guard house—and wait there until the time was right.

Chapter Seventeen

When Derek Vincannon reentered his dining room his wife and son were both sitting at the table.

"Where are the girls?" he asked.

"Upstairs," his wife answered.

He sat and said, "Well?"

"He's dangerous," Julie said.

"I agree," he said. "Jeremy?"

"I had Eric check on him, as you said, by telegraph," Jeremy Vincannon said. "He has a reputation. He is known as the Gunsmith."

"The Gunsmith," Vincannon said, frowning. "I've not heard of him. What is his reputation?"

"He is a deadly gunman," Jeremy said. "It is said that he has killed many men."

"I see," Derek Vincannon said.

"Why is he here?" Julie asked.

"He says he is not on his way to anywhere in particular," her husband said.

"What if he was?" she asked. "What if he was on his way here?"

"If that is the case," Derek Vincannon said, "then reputation or no, he will be sorry that he ever arrived."

The elder Vincannon turned to his son and said, "Watch him closely, Derek. If he goes to sleep, awakes in the morning and leaves, then let him. If he does anything else, let me know."

"I can take care—"

"Just let me know, Jeremy!" the father said tightly. "Do you understand? Do nothing on your own. Understand that?"

"Yes," the son said, "yes, Father, I understand."

Jeremy Vincannon left his father's house and stood right outside the door, seething. His *father's* house, that was not only the way he saw it, but the way his father saw it, as well.

And everyone else in Chance Awakening saw the settlement as his father's.

Jeremy Vincannon was tired of living under his father's roof, under his father's thumb.

He was more than ready to do something about it.

Derek Vincannon bade his wife good night and sat behind his desk with a cup of coffee. Chance Awakening was becoming more and more known to people riding through the area, and in a few more months it might even be enough of a curiosity to draw attention heavily.

Chance Awakening could become a full-fledged town very easily, if that was what the people wanted.

But the people wanted what Derek Vincannon wanted, and he *didn't* want Chance Awakening to become a town. He liked it better as a settlement.

He liked it better as *his* settlement, and if it became a town, it would cease to be his.

Chapter Eighteen

Clint Adams tried to go to sleep, but it was no use. It was just too damn early. Also, he was bothered by the existence of that telegraph key, and the question of why Derek Vincannon had lied about it.

Was Vincannon so afraid that the outside world would discover his little paradise, Chance Awakening? Or was it that he was afraid they would discover his little kingdom? Was he so much of a ruler here that people just went along with whatever he said? From what Clint could see, the settlement had a chance to really flourish into a town, if it was nurtured right—and if the United States Army gave up claim to the fort.

Clint had a deck of cards in his saddlebags. He took them out and, sitting at the dusty jailer's desk, dealt himself a couple of hands of poker.

He had played for half an hour, holding even on both sides, when there was a knock on the guard house door. Given the looks he'd been getting from Melissa Vincannon—he was almost certain he was going to have to fend her off.

However, when he opened the door it was another Vincannon entirely.

It was Jeremy.

"Hello, Jeremy."

"You're not asleep," Jeremy said.

"No."

"I didn't think you would be."

"It's still a little early."

Jeremy saw the cards dealt out on the desk.

"Ah, I see you like poker."

"I play from time to time."

"So do I."

"Your father doesn't sound like the kind of man who would condone gambling."

Jeremy rolled his eyes and said, "Oh, he's not, not anymore than he condones drinking or . . . or women of questionable morals."

"You don't have any women of questionable morals in the settlement, do you?" Clint asked.

"Not that I know of," Jeremy said, "more's the pity, but we do have some young men who enjoy a drink now and then, and a game of poker. I came over to see if you would be interested."

"In a drink, or poker?"

"Both," Jeremy said. "Some of us get together over at the hotel and play in the old dining room."

"Isn't that a little dangerous? I mean, your father's office is there."

"My father never goes to his office before nine A.M. and after seven P.M. We clean up afterward, and he never knows we were there. We're playing there tonight. Come along."

Clint was about to turn down the invitation, but then thought that it might sound suspicious if he did. Also, if there were a bunch of young men playing cards in the hotel, that was a little too close to where he thought the telegraph key was located.

If for no other reason than to know when their

game broke up he said, "All right, I could stand to play for a few hours."

"A few hours?" Jeremy said, laughing. "Sometimes we go almost all night!"

"Really?" Clint said, unhappily.

When they arrived at the hotel Clint saw that there were only three other men there, waiting for Jeremy and their guest player. One of the men was Vincent Tally, who did not look happy at Clint's arrival. The other two men were perfunctorily introduced as Dave and George. They were all in their mid-twenties.

"We have cards," Jeremy said, indicating the table, "and we have whiskey. Dave?"

Dave produced two bottles of whiskey and Jeremy explained that Dave and George were often dispatched to nearby towns to buy supplies, and made sure they stocked up on cards and whiskey.

"The only thing we don't do is smoke," Jeremy said. "My father would smell it, and besides, none of us smoke, anyway."

As they started the game Clint discovered something else these sheltered young men didn't do.

They didn't play poker very well.

And they didn't hold their liquor very well.

In an hour Clint had won most of the money they had started with—their raise limit was two bits—and three of the men—Dave, George and Vincent Tally—had fallen asleep at the table after consuming two glasses of whiskey each.

"They can't hold their likker!" Jeremy Vincannon said, slurring his words. He poured himself another shot glass, downed it, and promptly slammed his head down on the table.

Clint wondered, if this went on often enough, how long it would be before they wouldn't wake up in time to clear out before Derek Vincannon showed up in the morning.

He rose and checked each man carefully. There was no doubt but that they were passed out cold.

He'd never have a better opportunity to find that telegraph key than right now.

Chapter Nineteen

Clint left the hotel building and found the street deserted. All the nice, proper people of the settlement were in their beds for the night.

He stepped off the boardwalk and studied the buildings on either side of the hotel. Mentally retracing his steps of earlier he picked out the building he thought the sound of the telegraph key was coming from and approached it.

At one time it might have been a small shop of some kind, or might have actually been the telegraph office. He tried the front door and found it locked. There was a window next to the door and he tried to see through into the darkened interior, but he couldn't see anything. He was going to have to get inside the building, but breaking in through the front, even at this time of night, was too chancy.

He was going to have to try the back.

He walked along the boardwalk, looking for an alley that would lead him behind the buildings. He found one alley and wasted time following it to a dead end, then moved on and finally found an alley that went all the way through. He found himself behind the entire row of buildings, walked to the back of the hotel, then backtracked to the smaller building he wanted.

He tried the back door and found it locked. There

were no windows back here, and less chance of being heard if he had to damage the door.

He would have preferred not to damage the door, because then everyone would know that someone had been inside, and he would be the prime suspect, being the only stranger at the settlement.

He looked around the ground, and against the fence behind him and finally found what he wanted, a serviceable piece of wood. He was going to try and wedge it into the door and force the door open without cracking it or making it obvious that there was a break in.

He pushed the edge of the chunk of wood he was holding between the door and the door jamb and then began exerting pressure. The sound of cracking wood filled the air for a few seconds, but then the lock slipped and the door snapped open.

He discarded the piece of wood and stepped into the building, then closed the door behind him. It locked, which pleased him.

Now he wished he had a lamp of some kind. Not having one he stood stock still for a few moments while his eyes became accustomed to the more intense darkness inside.

Once his eyes started making out shapes he moved through the room, trying to find the key.

There were several tables, some of them covered with sheets, and he checked each table carefully but did not find the key.

Finished with the back room he moved through it to the front room. First he went to the window and looked out. Since it was so much darker inside, if there was anyone on the street he'd have been able to see them. He took a moment to hope that none of the young men next door had roused themselves yet.

He moved through the front room now and was disappointed not to find the key. He stood stock still with his hands on his hips and wondered if he could have picked out the wrong building. He didn't think so.

He went through the room again, and although he didn't find the key he did find a loose wire underneath a desk. He followed the wire up the wall where it disappeared through a small hole near the ceiling.

Whoever operated the key also apparently knew how to connect and disconnect it. Clint wondered if this was a matter of course, or if Derek Vincannon had instructed the operator to hide the key.

He wanted to go through both rooms again to see if it was hidden right there, but he decided not to take the time. The odds were good that if the key had been disconnected, it had also been taken away.

He left through the back door, tried the back door of the hotel and found it unlocked. It must have been the way Jeremy and his friends got into the hotel.

Inside, his plan was to go back to the dining room and see if he couldn't wake Jeremy and his friends and get them to go to bed. As he approached the four sleeping men—two of them were now snoring—he stopped without touching any of them. He turned, looked at the door to Derek Vincannon's office, and then figured, why not?

There were no windows in Vincannon's office, so Clint took a chance and lit the lamp on the man's desk. He went through Vincannon's desk drawers as carefully as possible and found a lot of personal papers that indicated that Vincannon might have still had some business connections back east—back east being Pennsylvania. He didn't have time to read the papers carefully and find out just what kind of business Vincannon was in, but it didn't appear that Derek Vincannon was really isolating himself totally at the settlement.

Clint searched the top of Vincannon's desk and came up empty. There was nothing here to tell Clint why he might have lied about the telegraph key— unless it was the way he kept in touch with business partners back east, and didn't want anyone else to know about that.

Maybe he wasn't as solidly entrenched as "ruler" as he would have liked.

Clint surveyed the desk to make sure he hadn't left anything grossly out of place, then doused the lamp and left the office.

In the dining room the four young men were still sprawled on the table, although one of them—he thought it was Dave—had slipped off somewhat and, given enough time, would soon slump off his chair and to the floor. Because of that Clint decided not to wake them. Let Dave do that when he fell off his chair.

Clint left the hotel building and made his way back to the compound. Keeping to shadows, he was reasonably sure he had made it back to the guard house without being seen.

He had also returned totally empty handed, which didn't please him at all.

Melissa Vincannon, her head slumped against the windowsill of her window, woke just in time to see the shadowy figure of Clint Adams moving across the compound. She knew it was him because she had paid attention to the way he moved when he was at the house for dinner, and no one else would have any reason to go to the guard house.

Also, it never occurred to her to wonder where Clint had been.

She was only glad that he was back, because he hadn't been there the first time she sneaked out of the house to see him.

She pulled on a robe and proceeded to sneak out of the house again.

Chapter Twenty

Now Clint was ready to go to sleep. As frustrated as he was at not being able to find the key, or any other helpful information, he was dog tired. It never occurred to him that it might be Melissa Vincannon, but it was.

"Hi," she said, stepping in past him without waiting for an invitation. "I didn't think you'd be asleep yet."

"What made you think that?" he asked, closing the door.

"I came by earlier, and you weren't here," she said.

"Oh," he said, "I went for a walk—"

She wasn't listening. She was too busy looking around the former guard house. He realized that she wasn't looking for any explanations.

"I've never been in here before."

"It isn't very interesting, I'm afraid," he said.

"Sure it is," she said, then she turned to stare boldly at him and said, "you're here."

Clint had removed his boots and shirt and was clad only in his jeans.

"Melissa, listen, I'm really ti—"

"You're leaving in the morning," she said.

"Probably—"

"If I let this chance go by I'd never forgive my-self," she said.

"Melissa—"

She moved closer to him and put her hands on his bare chest.

"All of the men around here are . . . boring," she said, "especially the young ones."

"That's too bad, but—"

"What I need is an older man, to teach me . . ." she said. She rubbed her hand over a spot on his chest, then leaned forward and kissed him. At the touch of her young lips he was suddenly not all that tired. "To show me . . ." she went on, rubbing an-other spot and kissing it.

"Melissa, your father—"

"My father is asleep," she said, "and he never wakes up until morning."

"Yes, but—"

"Don't you find me attractive?"

"I find you very attractive," he said, "*and* very young—"

"But that's what excites me about you," she said, getting up on her toes so she could kiss his neck. As though they had a mind of their own his hands went to her tiny waist. "You're older, you're attractive, and you've very experienced with women . . . aren't you?"

He could have said the same thing to her. She didn't seem as inexperienced as she might have led him to believe. Her mouth and hands certainly didn't *seem* to be eighteen years old.

"How old are you, Melissa?"

"I'll be nineteen next month," she whispered against the side of his neck. "Does that excite you, that I'm so much younger than you are?"

"Uh, yeah, I'd say that was a safe bet," Clint said, sliding his hands down from her waist to cup her firm buttocks.

She pressed herself tightly against him now, her arms going around his neck, her firm, round breasts flattening against his chest.

Unless he was wrong, she had nothing on underneath the robe.

"Melissa . . ."

"Yes?"

"Let me put out the lamp."

"All right."

She released him and he went to the desk and blew out the lamp. When he turned he couldn't see her in the darkness of the room.

"I'm in here . . ." he heard her voice call from the back. She was in one of the cells.

He walked into the cell block and almost tripped over something that was on the floor. He picked it up and found that it was her robe.

"Here . . ." she said, thinking he had lost her, again.

"I know . . ." he said, dropping the robe.

He moved to the cell she was in, paused to remove his pants, and then joined her.

She came to him and molded her firm, young body against his. Her flesh was unbelievably hot and again he cupped her buttocks. For a moment he thought that he shouldn't be doing this, but then he thought, what the hell. It had been a frustrating night, and why not enjoy a small part of it.

Her hungry mouth was moving over his chest, and when he was about to lift her chin to kiss her her mouth suddenly started a downward trail. When she found his rigid penis and took it in her mouth, he *definitely* knew that she was not inexperienced.

She worked him with her mouth, holding his balls in one hand, and holding the base of his cock with the other. Her head bobbed up and down and she moaned as she sucked him. He cupped her head and thought that this young woman really had him excited, because he felt he had no control over himself at all. In seconds he was exploding into her mouth, and she was having no problem accommodating his hot emission.

And that was just the beginning.

They moved to the cot next, and although there was not much room, they made the most of the space they had.

She climbed atop him and rubbed her wet pussy over his chest and belly before settling down and sliding onto him, taking him deep inside her with an animal growl. She began to rotate herself on him, bracing herself with her palms pressed down on his belly. He reached for her breasts, cupped them, squeezed the nipples, and she stopped moving and sat still on him. He pulled her down flat so he could suck her nipples and kiss her breasts. They were small, almost like peaches, but they were firm and round and her nipples were incredibly distended.

He also enjoyed the way her butt felt in his hands so much that he slid his hand down and cupped it again. She started to ride up and down on him, and he just held her and allowed her to dictate the momentum. She was amazingly wet, so much so that he felt her moisture on his thighs. She also had a sharp, clean young smell that he could almost taste, and it excited him so much that he decided that he *would* taste her.

He moved to his left, almost off the cot, so that he could slide her off of him onto the cot. As he moved off the cot he banged his knee painfully on the floor, but ignored the pain. He slid down between her legs and avidly began to lick her, tasting her and teasing her at the same time.

"Oh, God, yes," she said, reaching for his head and wrapping her hands in his hair. "At last, at last, a man who knows . . ."

She caught her breath when his tongue found her clit, and for the next few moments she was just moaning and crying out, writhing beneath him, and just for a moment he worried that someone might pass by and hear her, but then the moment passed and he made some noise of his own as he continued to lap at her with great enthusiasm.

"Ooh, God, please!" she said, finally. "Put it in me, get inside of me!"

He gave her one last, loving, long lick and then moved up over her. She spread her legs and her odor overwhelmed him. He poked into her and she was so wet he went straight to the core of her and she gasped and wrapped her legs around him.

"Hard, Clint," she said, "oh, ride me hard!"

He rode her hard, so hard that the cot threatened to collapse beneath them. Her breath was coming in great rasps as she clutched him to her, he felt her belly begin to tremble as her orgasm approached. He drove into her with even more vigor and at one point she said, "God, I'm . . . gonna . . . die!" and then she came, arching her back and nearly screaming . . .

Later he took her standing up. She was small enough for him to brace his legs and lift her onto his cock, and then stand there with her riding him, holding her butt as she bounced on him, biting his chin, licking his mouth, wetting his face. He could feel her fluid on his hands as she continued to ride him and he knew he'd feel some soreness in his legs tomorrow because she was small but heavier than she looked, but he didn't care, because right now what he was feeling was worth *any* pain that he had to pay for it with, and when he came, filling her with his seed, his legs almost collapsed beneath him, as if all of his strength was pouring out of him and into her . . .

Chapter Twenty-One

"Take me with you."

Clint Adams had slept with many women during his travels throughout the west. He knew that each time he did so he was taking the risk of hearing those exact words.

"Melissa—"

"I don't mean I expect you to marry me," she hurriedly added, "or that I expect you to stay with me. All I need is some transportation away from here."

"Why?" he asked. "Your family is here, this is your home."

"This has never been my home!" she said, bitterly. "I hate this place. I hated it when we first came here and I hate it even more now."

"But your family—"

"My family!" she said, her tone still bitter. "My father thinks only of his settlement, my brother thinks only of himself, my mother thinks of my father, and my sister . . ."

"Your sister?"

Melissa bit her lip as she stared at the ceiling of the cell and said, "Mara is the only one I'll miss, but I *have* to get out."

"That wouldn't be the proper way for me to repay your father's hospitality, Melissa."

"You call that hospitality? Sitting there and staring at you all during dinner, listening while the others questioned you?"

"He offered me shelter and food," Clint said. "That's hospitality."

"But he didn't give you what you wanted, did he?"

"And what was that?"

"The telegraph key."

He turned his head to look at her in the darkness. They were lying together on the cramped pallet and he could make out her profile in the darkness.

"How did you know about that?"

"I heard him telling Jeremy that you couldn't be allowed to find it."

"Why not?"

"I don't know," she said. "All I know is that he's hiding it from you." She looked at him now and said, "Who are you? Why are you really here?"

"I came here to use the telegraph key," he said. "I really can't tell you anymore than that."

"Why is my father afraid of you?"

"Is he?"

"I think so," she said. "I heard it in his voice when he was talking to Jeremy."

"Maybe he thinks I'm a threat to his life here at the settlement—and he may be right."

"What do you mean?"

"If I were to take you with me . . ."

She fell silent and thought about that, then said, "No, it's something else."

"What?"

"I don't know," she said, plaintively. "I don't

know why he's frightened of you, I only know that I want to leave . . ."

"Before you find out?"

"I don't know what you mean."

"Maybe you know what you're father is afraid of, Melissa," Clint said. "Maybe there's something going on here that he doesn't want anyone to know about."

"I don't know anything, Clint . . ." she said, getting up from the pallet and dressing.

"Melissa—"

"It was a mistake," she said. "Not coming here and being with you," she added hurriedly, "that was wonderful, but asking you to take me with you. That was a mistake. I apologize. Just forget I said anything."

"Melissa, do you know where the key is?"

She paused and then said, "Yes."

"Can you take me to it?"

She didn't answer.

"Melissa?"

"I have to think."

"I'm supposed to leave come morning," he said, "but I could arrange to stay—"

"I have to think," she said. "If you're still here . . ."

"Melissa—" he began, but she leaned over, kissed him quickly, and left.

He sat up on the pallet and thought for a few moments, then stood up and pulled on his pants. He wished he had a drink, that he had taken one of the bottles that Jeremy and his friends had had at the hotel.

He walked out to the desk and sat down. When he said to Melissa that something might be going on here, it suddenly occurred to him that *this* place could be the source of the trouble Kate and Jim West had been sent to look into. It didn't seem likely that a settlement of easterners could be the reason twenty-one people had disappeared, but it wasn't a possibility that could be ignored.

Now the question was, should he stay here and investigate the possibility when all he might be doing is wasting time?

Was the opportunity to send Cartwright a telegraph message worth the extra day?

Rubbing his jaw he knew that *something* was going on here. Granted, it could have nothing to do with the riddle he was searching the answer to, but there was really only one way to find that out.

He was going to have to stay.

Once again he slipped from the guard house, wondering if he was ever going to get any sleep tonight.

He found the livery and went inside. From the looks of it he was fairly certain that Vincannon would not be able to offer him a horse to replace his. All that remained was to hobble his horse without permanently laming him. He hated the thought of hurting the horse even a bit, but he needed a reason to stay. Luckily, it wasn't Duke.

He found his horse and leaned over to do the dirty deed with a sharp pebble he had picked up outside. When he was done he went back to the guard house and even as he went to sleep he could still hear the sound of the horse's discomfort as he gave him enough of a stone bruise to hobble him for a couple of days until it healed.

Come morning, Derek Vincannon was not going to be a happy man to have Clint Adams still around.

Chapter Twenty-Two

"I don't understand how this could be," Derek Vincannon said, looking distinctly unhappy.

"I don't either, Mr. Vincannon," Clint said, "but Jeremy saw it as well as myself."

Vincannon looked at Jeremy.

"It's true, Father," Jeremy said. "The horse has a stone bruise. He shouldn't be ridden."

"We could let you have one of ours—" Vincannon said.

"I'd much rather wait for my own—"

"—but we don't have any to spare," the man finished, and Clint fell silent.

They were standing in front of the Vincannon home. Derek and Jeremy were out front with Clint, while Julie was standing on the porch. Inside, at one of the windows, Clint could see both Mara and Melissa.

"I'm afraid I'll be your uninvited guest for a couple of more days, at least," Clint said.

"Uninvited," Vincannon said, his face expressionless, and then he smiled and said, "nonsense, of course you are invited. Come inside and my wife will serve you breakfast. Jeremy will see to the horse. Jeremy?"

Jeremy, looking unhappy and being relegated to liveryman, said, "Yes, Father."

"Come," Vincannon said, motioning Clint into his home.

Later, after breakfast, and after Clint Adams had announced that he was going to take a walk around the settlement, Derek Vincannon spoke to Jeremy in his office.

"What happened last night?"

"What do you mean, Father?"

Derek Vincannon, seated behind his desk, regarded his son with distaste.

"Jeremy, do you think I'm a fool?"

Jeremy Vincannon's stomach turned cold as he said, "W—what do you mean, Father?"

"Do you think I don't know what's been going on?"

Colder still, Jeremy said, "Father, I don't—"

"I'm talking about your little poker parties with your friends here in the dining room," Derek Vincannon said, stiffly.

"Oh," Jeremy said, breathing a sigh of relief but contriving to look apologetic. "That."

"Yes, that," Derek Vincannon said. "I've allowed it to go on because I felt you needed the outlet, but after what happened last night . . ."

"What happened last night?"

"That's what I want to know," Vincannon said.

"I don't know what—"

"Was Adams out of the guard house last night?"

Jeremy hesitated.

"It was your assignment to watch him."

"Well, yes, he was out—"

"Where did he go?"

"Here."

"Here?" Derek Vincannon said, looking down at his desk.

"Not in here," Jeremy said, hurriedly. "He was in the dining room with us, playing poker."

"And what did he do after you and your friends had drunk yourselves into a stupor?"

"I—he—"

"Someone broke in next door last night," the elder Vincannon said. "What do you suppose they were looking for, Jeremy?"

"Uh, the telegraph key?"

"And who among us would be looking for that?"

Jeremy shrugged and said, "None of us, Father."

"Then who?"

Jeremy's eyebrows went up as he said, "Adams?"

"Yes, Adams," Vincannon said, "and you and your friends made it easy for him."

"He didn't—"

"No, he didn't find it," Vincannon said, "but if he had . . ."

"If he had . . . what?"

"I don't know," Vincannon said. "He could have contacted someone."

"The army?"

"Perhaps."

"Father, you don't think the army would really want this place back?"

"I don't know what the army would want," Derek Vincannon said, "and I don't intend to ask them."

"But . . . what if they come?"

"We'll deal with that if and when it happens, Jeremy," Vincannon said. "Right now I want you to stop those wretched poker games, and the drinking."

"We only do it—"

"Even one time is too much, Jeremy," Vincannon said. "No more poker, and no more drinking."

Those activities were the least of his worries Jeremy agreed.

"Good. Now we must decide what to do about Adams."

"You think he lamed his own horse in order to stay and look for the telegraph key?"

"It's a possibility," Vincannon said. "The horse wasn't lame when he got here yesterday, was it?"

"No," Jeremy said, thinking back, "I unsaddled it, and it was fine."

"There you have it, then."

"Well, what do we do about it? What's he here for, Father?"

"I don't know. That question puzzles me, too. We have nothing here of great value that he could be after."

"Maybe you should let me and some of the others question him—"

"No!" Vincannon said. "No violence."

"Then what do you intend to do, just ask him?"

Derek Vincannon looked at his son and said, "You know, Jeremy, that may be the first decent idea you've had in some time."

Kate O'Hara strained against her bonds, but to no avail. She only succeeded in further chafing her already raw and sore wrists.

She was hungry. For some reason her meals had either been late in coming, or had been skipped. Because of it, she had lost count of the days she'd been there.

Where was Jim West? Surely, once she disappeared, Cartwright would send Jim in to find her?
And what if he had, and Jim had met the same fate
that she had? Or worse yet, been killed?

Who would come looking for her then?

Chapter Twenty-Three

Clint's walk around the settlement told him very little. In general the people were very friendly, more so than in any town he'd ever been in. Their good humor and good nature was unreserved, which was odd. Perhaps Vincannon actually *did* have something here worth lying for.

Walking back towards the compound he saw Mara Vincannon coming towards him. When she saw him she smiled and changed her course to intersect with his.

"Good morning, Clint," she greeted with a smile. It transformed her face from simply lovely to absolutely beautiful. He couldn't think of any other word for it. Thinking of her and her sister made him think twice about the settlement as a paradise. It was a shame that two such young women had to be locked away where no one else could see them, where they wouldn't be able to blossom and flourish as they grew to full womanhood.

"Good morning, Mara. You look exceptionally lovely today."

"Oh," she said, as if taken aback by the compliment. Maybe she didn't receive her fair share while locked away here. "Thank you."

"Where are you off to?"

"Just taking a walk," she said, then blushed and

119

lowered her head, as if caught in a lie. "No," she said, then, confessing, "that's a lie. I was looking for you."

"For me?" he asked, wondering if Melissa had said anything to her sister about last night. "I'm very flattered."

She blushed again. He wondered if it was the younger sister who had all the experience with men and compliments.

"I . . . wanted to talk with you."

"About what?"

"About . . . the outside."

"The outside," Clint said, sadly. "Is that what you call it?"

"What else can I call it?" she said. "I've known nothing but this place for almost five years."

Again he considered the shame of it.

"Why don't we walk a while?" he asked.

"Will you tell me about . . . other places?" she asked. "All the places you've been to?"

He smiled, took her arm and said, "I'll tell you anything you want to know, Mara."

Clint and Mara walked together from one end of the settlement to the other for the better part of an hour. Finally, as they approached the gates to the compound again, Jeremy Vincannon and Vincent Tally spotted them.

"Look at that," Tally said.

"What about it?" Jeremy said.

"He's walking with Mara," Tally said, as if it signaled the end of the world.

"So what? We've got more important things to worry about, Vincent."

"You maybe," Tally said. "She's your sister. I don't have such blood ties to her."

"Are you still hoping she'll marry you?" Jeremy asked. "Forget it, Vincent—"

"I'll see you later," Tally said, and started towards Clint and Mara.

"Vincent—" Jeremy said, but Tally was gone.

Jeremy decided to watch.

"Thank you, Clint," Mara said. She didn't see Tally approaching and reached up to plant a chaste kiss on Clint's cheek.

Tally, seeing this, became incensed.

"Mara!" he shouted.

She turned and saw Tally, his rifle in his hand, approaching them.

"Oh, no . . ." she said.

"Mara . . ." Clint said.

"Mara!" Tally said again.

"Vincent . . ." she said, warningly. "Don't . . ."

"Tally . . ." Clint said.

For a moment Tally was undecided who to go after, Mara or Clint. In the end he made his decision and grabbed hold of Mara's arm roughly.

"What are you doing with him?"

"Vincent . . ." she gasped, "you're hurting me . . ."

"Answer me!" Tally shouted, shaking her.

"Tally!" Clint snapped. "Let her go!"

"Mind your own business, Adams!" Tally said. "This is between Mara and me."

"Mara?" Clint asked.

"Make him let go," she said to Clint. "Please."

"Mara—" Tally said.

"Tally," Clint said again, sharply. When Tally

turned to look at him again Clint stepped in and hit him on the jaw.

The younger man staggered back, releasing Mara so suddenly that she staggered and would have fallen if Clint had not grabbed her around the waist.

Tally fell to the ground, sprawling in the sand. He looked up and saw Clint standing there with his arm around Mara. He grabbed for the rifle in the sand but, as his hand closed over it, a foot came down on his hand.

"Don't be a fool, man," Derek Vincannon said. "He'll kill you."

"Let me go!"

"Enough!" Vincannon said.

He removed his foot and picked up the rifle.

"Get up and clean yourself off, Tally," Vincannon said.

Tally, feeling embarrassed and angry, got to his feet and brushed himself off.

"I'll give you this back, but you have to go right to the front gate," Vincannon said.

"But he and Mara—"

"Oh, be quiet," Vincannon said. He tossed Tally the rifle and said, "Go to the front gate, Vincent, and stop this foolishness."

Tally glared at the three of them in turn, then stalked away into the compound.

Derek Vincannon turned and looked at his daughter and Clint, who slid his protective arm from her waist.

"Mara, go home."

"Father, it was Vincent—"

"I know what happened," her father said. He nodded to her and said, "Go on home."

"Yes, Father."

She gave Clint a quick look, managing to convey both gratitude and apology.

"Will you come with me to my office?" Vincannon asked Clint.

"For what reason?"

"To talk."

"About this?"

Vincannon made an impatient gesture with his hand.

"I couldn't be less concerned about what took place here. We have to talk about something else. Will you accompany me?"

"Lead the way," Clint said.

Maybe they were about to get to the truth.

He hoped.

Jeremy Vincannon had witnessed the entire incident, and now watched his father and Clint Adams walk off in the direction of the hotel. He wondered if his father was really going to flat out ask Adams what he was doing here? What did he think Adams was going to do, tell the truth?

He thought about what a fool his father was sometimes.

He thought about what a fool Vincent Tally was, his friend, his right hand. He was going to have to make sure Vincent had his priorities straight.

He went into the compound to find Tally and rescue him from his menial task for something more important.

Chapter Twenty-Four

In Vincannon's office Clint was surprised to see that the man had a bottle of whiskey on his desk, with two glasses.

"I thought you might like a drink," Vincannon said. "Would you like one?"

"Sure," Clint said, "I could do with a drink."

"I appropriated this from where my son has them hid. He thinks I don't know about them."

Vincannon poured out two shot glasses and passed one to Clint's side of the desk. He sat down behind his desk with the other in hand.

"What did you want to talk to me about?" Clint asked.

"Several things," Vincannon said. "For one thing, someone broke into the building next door last night."

"Really? Does that happen often around here?"

"It happens not at all," Vincannon said, "which is why I know it was you."

Clint didn't respond. He was sure Jim West would have had some quick return.

"You were looking for the telegraph key," Vincannon went on. "Apparently you didn't believe me when I told you it wasn't in working order."

Clint sipped his drink.

"I had hoped we could be frank with each other," Vincannon said.

"If that's the case," Clint said, "I suggest you start."

Vincannon smiled a genuine smile for the first time since Clint had met him.

"You are the guest."

If the man was truly ready to be honest, then Clint was sorry that he had to continue to lie about certain things.

"All right," he said, putting his glass down on the desk. "I did break in, and I was looking for the telegraph key."

"Why?"

"Yesterday, when Tally was bringing me here, I heard the key being used. I knew it worked, you see, so I knew you were lying."

Vincannon nodded and said, "I see."

"Why were you lying?"

Vincannon put his glass down on the desk. He still had not drunk any. He passed his hand over his gray hair, composing his thoughts.

"I believe I told you how much the settlement means to us," he said, finally, "to me. Probably more to me than to anyone else, I admit. And perhaps I am overprotective of it, and of the people."

"And," Clint found himself saying, "perhaps not."

"What do you mean?"

"On one hand I find the people here very friendly —except for Tally, of course, but he has his reasons."

"Jealousy," Vincannon said, smiling for real again. "The poor boy doesn't realize that Mara is not interested in him. He refuses to believe that."

"He'll have to accept it sooner or later."

Vincannon waved his hand and said, "We are not here to discuss my family matters. Please, continue what you have to say."

"Only that the people seem to be very content here, with only a few exceptions."

He hoped that Vincannon would not ask him who those exceptions were, right now.

"I'm glad you can see that," the older man said. "Perhaps, if you had any thoughts of . . . of doing something to change that . . ."

"That's not why I came here, Mr. Vincannon," Clint said. "I didn't know about Chance Awakening, and now that I do I have no desire to . . . to ruin it for you."

"Why did you come here, then?"

"As I said originally," Clint said, "I came looking for a telegraph key."

"To send a message to your uncle."

"Yes."

Vincannon picked up his drink, downed it and then returned the glass to the desk. The move told Clint that the man had not been a teatotaler all his life.

"I was a businessman in the east, Mr. Adams," he said, then. "In fact, I maintain interest in some of my businesses. Others I sold outright. I am a fairly wealthy man and could probably live anywhere in the world if I wanted to."

"You chose here."

"I wanted to take my family away from . . . from the cruelty that seems to have become accepted in every day society, both in the east and the west. I want to . . . to shelter them." Clint started to speak, but Vincannon stopped him with a hand movement. "My point is that my desire to shelter my family does not mean that I am naive. I lived in the so-called real world for many years, and did quite well for myself. I'm *not* a fool, and I don't for one minute believe that you altered your course to find a telegraph key to contact your uncle. I'm sorry, sir."

"I'm sorry, too," Clint said, "but I can't tell you anymore. I can only tell you that I would like to use that key."

"You expect me to trust you."

"I don't expect it, no," Clint said, "but I would like you to, yes."

"A tall order, sir," Vincannon said, "a very tall order, and one that requires a lot of thought."

Clint remained silent.

"And your horse's injury?" Vincannon said.

"Ah, that was something unforeseen, I'm afraid," Clint said. He did not want to admit to that, because it could have led back to the fact that he had seen Melissa last night. He could also see that Vincannon didn't believe that, either.

Trust was very hard to come by, especially if you were doing nothing to earn it.

Well, Clint wasn't totally convinced that Vincannon was being completely frank and open with him, either.

And maybe Clint Adams was just one of those people who Derek Vincannon was trying to shelter his family from.

"If your father finds out I'm not at my post—" Vincent Tally said.

"He *and* Clint Adams just made a total fool of

you, Vincent, and you're worried about getting *him* angry? Vincent, you'd better smarten up."

"What do you mean?"

"Clint Adams is a major threat to everything we have here. You know what that means?"

"What?"

"He has to go."

"How do we get him to leave?"

"No," Jeremy said patiently, shaking his head, "I don't mean he has to leave, I mean he has to *go* . . . *permanently* . . . as in dead."

"You mean . . . kill him?"

"Exactly," Jeremy said, like a teacher complimenting a reticent student who had finally learned his lesson.

Chapter Twenty-Five

"For whatever reason, it seems you'll be here two more days, at least," Vincannon said from behind his desk. "I'll have to think about your request, Mr. Adams."

"I don't understand—"

"Neither do I, sir," Vincannon said, "which is precisely why I need time to think."

"Very well," Clint said, after a moment.

He stood up, went to the office door, and left. He had hoped Vincannon would have something else to say before he left, but the man did not stop him.

Clint walked through the dining room, into the lobby, and to the front door.

On the roof of the hotel Vincent Tally stood with his rifle ready. Jeremy had explained it to him, and it all made sense. In addition, killing Adams would get him out of the way so that Tally could finally marry Mara.

He waited, sighting down the barrel of the rifle, for Clint Adams to step into the street.

Clint stepped out of the hotel and paused there a moment. If Vincannon was just what he appeared to be, a patriarchal figure trying to protect his family and his neighbors, then he felt badly about lying. Whatever the danger was in this "Arizona Triangle"

Chance Awakening was right in the middle of it.

On the other hand, *was* Chance Awakening right in the middle of it?

Tally's heart was pounding, and when he saw Clint Adams' back he almost jumped out of his boots. He fixed his grip on the rifle again, because his hands were sweating, and then he jerked the trigger.

He jerked it, he did not pull it.

That cost him his life.

At the sound of the shot Clint threw himself to the ground, rolling. The move saved his life, but he felt the bullet strike him in the left shoulder. He came up on one knee with his gun in his hand. He saw Tally on the roof, setting himself for a second shot, and didn't give him a chance to make it.

Clint fired once and Tally staggered, dropped the rifle, staggered again and then fell off the roof to the street below.

Clint didn't have to check him to know he was dead, and he had no time to feel sorry for having to kill the man. Tally had tried to shoot him in the back. As far as Clint Adams was concerned, that was the worst thing a man could do, and as far as he was concerned, Vincent Tally was better off dead.

Clint was standing over Tally when Derek Vincannon came out of the hotel, along with a mob of people from the other buildings in the area. He ejected the used shell from his modified Colt and reloaded, then holstered it.

". . . happened?" someone asked.

". . . heard shots . . ."

". . . who's dead . . ."

". . . who's that . . ."

Clint ignored the people around him and concentrated on Vincannon, who looked down at Tally with a sad look on his face, and then back at Clint. He saw that Clint was bleeding from the shoulder.

"You're hurt."

"Is there a doctor in this . . . place?"

"Yes, his office is above the general store."

Clint turned to leave, then turned back to Vincannon and said, "Could he have been that jealous, Vincannon? Or did someone put him up to trying to back shoot me?"

Vincannon looked up at Clint, a puzzled look in his eyes.

"What do you mean?"

"I mean he tried to kill me by shooting me in the back," Clint said. "He would have, too, if he wasn't such a bad shot. Did he do that simply because your daughter Mara took a walk with me?"

"I . . . don't know . . ." Vincannon said, apparently at a loss to explain.

"Well, I'll find out," Clint said, "and when I do, I just might pull your little paradise down around your ears, Vincannon."

Clint walked away towards the doctor's office, people passing him on the run to see what had happened.

He already regretted his last words to Vincannon. If the man ever thought he was a threat to the well being of Chance Awakening and its people, it was now.

He was going to have to watch his back very carefully the rest of the time he was there.

Jeremy Vincannon heard the shots from his father's house and knew that Tally had failed.

"What was that?" Julie Vincannon said, her head whipping around.

"A shot, Mother."

"Jeremy—"

"I'll go and check on Father, Mother," Jeremy said.

He heard his sisters rush down the steps to talk to their mother as he left the house and walked slowly across the compound.

Chapter Twenty-Six

As Clint approached the doctor's office he saw the door open and a young man came bounding down the steps. He recognized him as Dave Hopkins, one of the young men he'd played poker with.

He waited until Hopkins left, then mounted the steps and climbed to the second floor, where the doctor's office was. When he reached the door there was a shingle on the wall next to it that said: Doctor Emmett P. Hopkins.

He introduced himself to the doctor and told him what happened. Dr. Hopkins instructed him to take off his shirt.

Dr. Hopkins was a man about Derek Vincannon's age, a painfully thin man with thinning gray hair.

"Did you hear the shots?" Clint asked as the doctor examined his shouder.

"I did."

"Weren't you curious?"

The doctor shrugged.

"I felt it was more important I stay here, where I could be found."

"That's a pretty cavalier attitude towards shooting. I understood that sort of thing didn't happen around here?"

"There are other kinds of injuries than bullet

135

wounds, Mr. Adams, although I suspect a man such as yourself wouldn't know that."

"What do you know about the kind of man I am?"

"Word gets around."

"Well, don't believe everything you hear—ouch!"

The doctor finished cleaning the wound and said, "You were lucky. The bullet creased you and kept on going. I'll bandage it. I wouldn't advise any sudden moves for a while, or you'll start it bleeding again."

"I'll keep that in mind."

When the doctor was finished Clint put his shirt back on and asked how much he owed.

"Nothing."

"What do you mean, nothing?"

"As I understand it, you are a guest of this settlement. No charge."

Clint was going to argue further, then decided against it.

"Thank you, Doctor."

"Think nothing of it."

Clint started for the door, then stopped and said, "The young man leaving as I arrived. Who is he?"

"My son, David," the man answered over his shoulder, then turned and asked, "Why?"

"No reasons," Clint said. "Just curious."

He left, heading back to the compound. He wanted to get a clean shirt from his saddlebags, and think about what had happened.

He wanted to try and put everything into its proper perspective.

In light of the attempt on his life there was no longer any doubt that something was going on in the alleged paradise of Chance Awakening. The question, still remained, however, if it had any connection with the missing people.

Also, if Derek Vincannon had no connection with the attempt, then someone else in Chance Awakening was wielding some authority. Clint had the feeling there was a power struggle going on here, and maybe Derek Vincannon didn't even know it.

Clint was in the guardhouse and had just donned a clean shirt when there was a knock on the door. He opened it and found himself facing a man he'd never seen before.

"Mr. Vincannon would like to see you in his office, Mr. Adams," the man said, "if it's convenient."

So Vincannon had replaced Tally already, this time with a polite version. By the looks of the rifle in the man's hand, it might even have been the same one Tally had been carrying.

"All right," Clint said, "tell Mr. Vincannon I'll be along shortly."

"All right, sir."

Clint closed the door. Although it was Vincannon who was sending for him, it was *he* who was going to make some demands.

Clint knocked on the door to Vincannon's office and it was opened by the same man who had come to fetch him.

"It's Mr. Adams, sir," the man said.

"All right, John," Vincannon said. "Leave us alone."

Clint entered the room and the man called John slid past him and closed the door on his way out. When Clint looked at the man behind the desk he was shocked at what he saw.

Vincannon seemed to have grown older in the past hour, since the shooting. His hair was a mess, as if he had been raking it with his fingers. His eyes appeared sunken, his skin lined and dry. What was a further shock was that the whiskey bottle on the desk was now only half full.

"Mr. Vincannon?"

The man looked up at Clint and waved an arm in what might have been a motion of surrender.

"John is waiting outside to take you to the telegraph key, Adams," Vincannon said.

"Why the sudden change of heart?"

"Something is happening here and I don't know what it is," Vincannon said, "and it's beyond my experience to deal with it. I'm going to ask you for help, once you've sent your telegraph message. I'm hoping that you will give it to me, but I don't expect you to."

"Derek—"

"Go on," Vincannon said, "send your message. We can talk afterward."

Clint hesitated, then left without saying thank you. After all, Vincannon was only allowing him to use the key for his own reasons.

John took Clint next door, to the building he'd broken into. The key had been set up again, and the operator was there, waiting. He was an older man, in his sixties, but his eyes were strong and his hands were steady.

"All I need is a refresher," Clint told him, "and I'll be able to send the message myself."

The man shrugged, gave Clint the refresher and then he and John left the room.

Clint wanted to be frank in his message, but he also wanted to keep it short. He tried some practice runs, found his fingers tripping over each other, and then tried again more slowly. Finally, he felt ready to send the message.

It came out this way:

W.M.C.

ARRIVED AND DEPARTED MESA SAFELY. AM ON TO SOMETHING. WILL KEEP IN TOUCH.

C.A.

It was concise and to the point. He had arrived and left Mesa safely, and he was on to something. He could only hope that he wasn't wasting time in Chance Awakening while Kate O'Hara, West and others weren't suffering somewhere—if they weren't all dead.

He secured the key and went to tell the operator that he could have it back. Then he told John he wanted to go back to Vincannon's office, and that he could find his own way.

"All right, sir," the polite John said, and Clint entered the hotel.

Derek Vincannon felt confused.

He was surprised that one act of violence could unnerve him so, destroy his resolve that he was doing absolutely the right thing for his family, the people of Chance Awakening... and, of course, himself.

Now, he wasn't sure of anything. A man had been

killed in Chance Awakening, which now made it no different than any other place in the world.

He opened his bottom drawer and took out a .41 caliber Colt Cloverleaf revolver. He was contemplating it when Clint Adams walked in.

Clint looked at Vincannon for a moment and then said softly, "What would that accomplish?"

Vincannon looked at Clint with haunted eyes. The gun rested on the desk, but it was still in his hands.

"I've failed."

"So?" Clint said. "Is it the first time?"

"No."

"And will it be the last?"

Vincannon didn't answer.

"No, Derek, it won't be the last," Clint said. He approached the desk and took the gun from Vincannon's nerveless hands. He unloaded it, then dropped the shells into his pocket and the gun onto the desk.

"Let's talk."

This time, Clint decided, it was time to be completely frank.

Chapter Twenty-Seven

Clint told Vincannon exactly why he was there, and if it was possible, Vincannon looked even worse for it.

"You can't possibly think that we here at Chance Awakening could have anything to do with . . . that?" he asked, horrified.

"Can you say, without a shadow of a doubt—in light of what's happened—that no one here has anything to do with it?"

"Yes!" Vincannon answered, defiantly.

"Derek, if I had told you that someone here would try to kill me before I left, would you have believed me?"

"N-no . . . no, I would not have," Vincannon said, and the defiance was gone, replaced once again by uncertainty and doubt.

"Tell me about Vincent Tally."

"Vincent traveled here with us from the east. He was not . . . I did not approve of him for Mara, but she was the reason he came. Even then he loved her, and they were just children. He asked if he could come along and I said he could."

"Why, if you didn't approve of him."

"I said I didn't approve of him for Mara. He is— was a dependable worker, a strong worker, and he obeyed orders—most of the time."

"Then why did you not approve of him?"

"He wasn't strong enough for Mara," Vincannon said. "Oh, he was strong enough in the physical sense, but he was too easily led. He was a follower, not a leader, and Mara needs a strong hand. She needs her man to be a leader."

"Like her father."

"Yes," he said, laughing ironically, "I have certainly been a fine leader, haven't I?"

Clint cursed himself silently for the remark. He was completely convinced that whatever was going on in Chance Awakening was going on without the knowledge of Derek Vincannon.

"All right, let's get back to Tally. If he was easily led, then who led him? Besides you?"

Vincannon only had to think a moment before replying, "Jeremy."

"Your son."

"Yes. Vincent looked up to Jeremy. In the beginning Vincent had hoped that Jeremy could convince Mara to marry him, but then he thought Jeremy became his friend."

"And he didn't?"

Vincannon looked Clint straight in the eye.

"My son has no friends, Clint," he said. "Remember when I said Vincent was a leader? Well, Jeremy is not only a leader, he's a user. He befriends people, makes them think he's their friend, so he can use them."

"If he's such a leader, why do you assign him menial tasks?"

"I had hoped that he would change, learn humility, become a *true* leader, but it has not been working."

"This is going to be a difficult question for you to answer, Derek."

"Go ahead and ask it," Vincannon said. "It can't be any more difficult than everything else that I've had to face today."

"If your son told Vincent Tally to kill me, would he have done it?"

Without hesitation Vincannon replied, "Yes. Jeremy would have been able to convince Vincent of anything—even murder."

"You're sure of that?"

"I've always been sure, I've just never faced up to it."

Clint told Vincannon that he now suspected Jeremy of planning to usurp his authority eventually.

"All he'd have to do is get himself enough followers like Vincent Tally. Are there enough of them here?"

"You've met some of them," Vincannon said. "You played poker with them."

"Those two? Dave, and . . . what was it, George?"

"Dave Hopkins and George Fredricks. They joined us soon after we left Pennsylvania. They were cousins who were traveling together. They fancy themselves a 'gang,' the type they read about in dime novels."

"Jeremy, Vincent, Dave and George," Clint said, ticking them off on his fingers. "Who else?"

"I don't know—maybe half a dozen others who would follow Jeremy if he told them to."

"With eight armed men Jeremy could take over this settlement and receive very little resistance, wouldn't you say?"

"Yes," Vincannon said, "God help us, yes. I convinced the others of the need to control who had arms and who didn't."

"And the men with the arms, the men you have manning the walls, they're Jeremy's 'gang,' aren't they?"

"They weren't all in the beginning," Vincannon said, "but I believe they are now, yes."

"Are there other guns in town?"

"Yes, in the old sheriff's office."

"Let's go and take a look, Derek," Clint said. "We may need them before we're through."

"Yes, all right," Vincannon said, standing up.

"Wait," Clint said.

He picked up the Cloverleaf, reloaded it and handed it to Vincannon. The older man looked at it in his hand for a few moments, then tucked it awkwardly into his belt.

Vincannon led Clint to the old sheriff's office and used a key to open the door. When they entered Clint heard Vincannon's sharp intake of breath.

It didn't take a genius to figure out what the problem was. Clint could see for himself that the gun rack was empty and, judging by the amount of dust covering it, it had been for some time.

"Looks like Jeremy and his boys got here first," Clint said.

"I can't believe this," Vincannon said.

"You'd better start believing it," Clint said, "because we've got to do something about it, and fast. I've got to find out if Jeremy is just playing Jesse James, or if he's behind these disappearances. If he's not, I've still got my work to do."

"Yes, you're right," Vincannon said. "You could be wasting your time here."

"I could," Clint replied, but somehow, he thought, I don't think I am.

"Derek, I'll need the key to this place," he said.

"What for?"

"I think I may be getting some use out of this place soon."

Vincannon hesitated a moment, then handed over the key.

"We'll need men we can rely on, Derek," Clint said, accepting it. "Are there any?"

"Yes, there are some," Vincannon said, frowning. He was already formulating a list in his head.

"And they'll have to supply their own weapons."

"I . . . don't know what they'll have," Vincannon said, "but we can try."

"Derek," Clint said, indicating the empty gun rack which had probably once held an equal number of rifles and shotguns, "we have to do a hell of a lot more than try."

Chapter Twenty-Eight

"What's the problem, Jeremy?" Dave Hopkins asked.

Jeremy stared at Hopkins as if he were crazy.

"You know what happened earlier today, Dave," he said, "and you can still ask me what the problem is?"

He looked at each of the others in turn, Fredricks, Wayne Garrett, Steve Granger, Andy Fry and the Orlow brothers, Frank and Jimmy. They were meeting where they always did, in an abandoned building at the southern end of the settlement. It was here that they had discovered the tunnels.

"You all know what the problem is," Jeremy said. "You've known for some time. You know about the other two people the government sent, and you know that now they've sent a living legend, the Gunsmith himself."

"The Gunsmith?" Steve Granger said. "You mean that fella who got here yesterday?"

"Clint Adams," Jeremy said, "the Gunsmith, himself."

Many of them had read the dime novels about the Gunsmith and were shocked that the man had jumped off the pages of those novels and into their lives.

"And you sent Vincent to kill him? Alone?" George Fredricks asked.

"That was my mistake," Jeremy admitted, "sending him alone. We'll all have to go against him next time. He can't kill all of us."

"He'll get some of us," Jimmy Orlow pointed out.

"Probably," Jeremy said.

They all exchanged looks now, none of them looking at Jeremy Vincannon.

"Listen to me!" Jeremy snapped, and they all looked at him then. "We're in this together and nobody can back out now. Even if you do, and we go down, you'll go down with us, so backing out does you no good."

"But . . ." Wayne Garrett said.

"But what?"

"It'll be murder."

"That it will be," Jeremy said. "Just like it was the first time."

"That was an accident!" Andy Fry cried out.

They all looked at Andy. It had been he who had taken a liking to that first woman and decided to rape her. The others had followed suit afterward, but it had been Andy's idea. They all knew that.

They also knew that by the time the last of them had their way with her, the woman was dead. Her husband went crazy, and they had to kill him. And then the boy . . .

"That's what we call it, Andy," Jeremy said. "What do you think the law will call it?"

"Murder," Frank Orlow said. "They'll call it murder, for sure."

"That's right," Jeremy said. "And don't forget about the others . . ."

"But Jeremy," Steve Granger said, "we're not gunmen, none of us."

"That doesn't matter," Jeremy said, "because when we get him, he won't even see it coming."

"How you gonna work that?" Jimmy Orlow asked.

"I'm going to get some help," Jeremy Vincannon said.

"From who?" Fredricks asked.

Jeremy smiled and said, "A most unlikely source —one of my sisters."

"Your sisters?" Wayne Garrett asked.

"Which one?" Fredricks asked.

"It doesn't matter," Jeremy said. "Like any man —like all of you—he's got a yen for them both. I just have to decide which one."

"And then tell her what?" Fredricks asked. "That you need her help killing the Gunsmith?"

"Don't be stupid, George," Jeremy said. "Whether it's Mara or Melissa, she won't know any more than he does."

"And when he's dead?" Fredricks asked. "What is she going to do then?"

"Nothing," Jeremy said. "By then I'll be the leader of this settlement, and they'll all do as I say. Things are going to change around here, boys. We're going to become a real town, and we're going to be the town fathers. We've been hampered by my father's shortsightedness long enough. It's time to make our move."

"Even if it means murder," George Fredricks said.

"Yes," Jeremy said, looking at each of them in turn, "even if it means murder. There probably isn't a town in the West that wasn't built on a foundation of blood. Abilene, Dodge City, Laredo, Tombstone, all of the great towns, and now us!"

They all saw the mad glint in his eyes, and they all turned away from it.

"This was fun when we was just play-acting," Jimmy Orlow said to his brother, Frank. At eighteen, Jimmy was the youngest potential "founding father." It was also Jimmy, going last, who had been on top of the woman when she shuddered and died. "Now this is serious."

"I know."

"None of us knows nothing about this kind of stuff, except what we read."

"Try and tell him that," Frank Orlow said, jerking his chin towards Jeremy.

They were outside now, and Jeremy was talking with George Fredricks and Wayne Garrett in front of their "hideout."

"He's crazy, Frank," Jimmy said.

"I know, Jimmy," Frank Orlow said, "I know, but we're in too deep to back out now."

"Way too deep," Jimmy said, agreeing, and hating it.

He could still feel that woman dying beneath him.

Chapter Twenty-Nine

"This is still too fantastic for me to completely believe," Derek Vincannon said.

Clint Adams, seated across the desk from him, stared at Vincannon.

"Talk it out, Derek," he said.

Vincannon leaned forward and said, "Don't you think I, or someone, would have noticed if nineteen people were being held captive here?"

"Twenty-one," Clint said, "and if you haven't noticed, what does that indicate to you?"

"That they're not here!"

"There's another possibility," Clint said softly.

"What?"

"Think about it."

Vincannon took a moment, then sat back in his seat as it hit him.

"You mean . . . they were . . . killed."

Clint nodded.

"You expect me to believe that my son killed twenty-one people?"

"Or had it done," Clint said. "Isn't that the way you said he'd have done it?"

"I didn't—"

"You said he was a leader, and used people, and could get them to do things."

As his own words came back at him Derek Vincannon winced as each one hit him like a blow to the head.

"When are these people going to get here?" Clint asked.

He'd given Vincannon an hour to round up whatever men he thought he could rely on.

"An hour?" Vincannon had complained.

"This has to be resolved very soon, Derek," Clint said, "tonight, if possible."

In the end he had agreed, and had gone to talk to some people.

"They'll be here soon."

"How many?"

Vincannon stared straight ahead of him, and apparently had not heard the question.

"Derek, how many?" Clint asked again.

"Oh, I'm sorry . . . I don't know how many will come, but I spoke to a dozen."

"A dozen," Clint said. "In sheer numbers it should be enough. It might even deter your son and his . . . his gang."

Clint wondered if a group of rank amateurs could really be behind a batch of disappearances that had attracted the attention of the United States Secret Service, and if so what the hell was behind it?

What was Chance Awakening sitting on?

Oil?

Minerals?

Treasure?

What?

Jimmy and Frank Orlow were walking across the street from the hotel when they saw three men enter the hotel together.

"What's going on over there, I wonder?" Jimmy said.

"I don't know," Frank, the elder by four years, said, "but maybe we ought to tell Jeremy about it. Come on."

There was a knock on the office door and Clint rose to answer it. He admitted three men to the room. Not one of them was under fifty-five, if he was any judge of age.

Still . . .

"Curt Stark, Sam Jordan and Russell King," Vincannon said, making the introductions. "Gentlemen, Clint Adams."

"Glad to meet you gents," Clint said. "We brought some chairs in from the dining room for you. Make yourselves comfortable while we wait for the others."

One of them, Russell King, looked at Vincannon and said, "There won't be any others, Derek."

"What do you mean?"

"He means we're it," Sam Jordan said. "The others you spoke to aren't coming."

"Why not?"

"This isn't their kind of fight, Derek," Curt Stark said.

"As a matter of fact, it's not ours either, but . . ." Russell King said.

"But it's their to—I mean, settlement, too," Clint said. "How can they not—"

"Mr. Adams—or Mr. Gunsmith, I don't know what to call you," Jordan said.

"Adams will do."

"Fine. Mr. Adams, you have lived by your gun

most of your life. We, and the others, are merchants, store owners. The most strenuous thing we've done in our lives is load supplies. A gun? The three of us fought in the war, we used guns then, maybe we still remember how. The others? They'd shoot their foots off, or worse."

"But a show of force—"

"A bunch of old men against Jeremy's young bucks?" Sam Jordan said. "What kind of show of force would that be."

"Derek," Russell King said, "we're surprised you didn't know before this."

"Know what?" Vincannon asked.

Clint had a feeling that Derek Vincannon was about to hear something that would shatter his already shaken confidence.

"About Jeremy," Clint heard Curt Stark say as he went through the door, "he's been talking to some of us for a while now, about changes . . ."

Changes, Clint thought, as he walked through the dining room.

Wasn't that just what Derek Vincannon had been afraid of all this time, and now it was coming on to haunt him—brought about by his own son.

Clint left the hotel, doubting that he'd be able to depend on anyone else for help. By virtue of their numbers, even though they were inexperienced, Jeremy and his followers—he couldn't keep thinking of them as a "gang"—had the upper hand.

He had to find a way to reverse that.

Jimmy Orlow saw Clint Adams leave the hotel and his heart started beating faster. He'd read every dime novel that had been written about the Gunsmith, and now there he was, big as life.

Jimmy was supposed to watch the building and keep count of who went in and out. Well, he hadn't seen anyone else enter, and now the Gunsmith was leaving.

The Gunsmith, he thought in awe, and stepped out of the doorway he'd been standing in to get a better look at a living legend.

Clint saw the boy even before he stepped out of the doorway. He couldn't have been more than eighteen. Could he be one of Jeremy Vincannon's followers? If so, how many of the others were like him?

Could Jeremy Vincannon and eight or nine disciples like this one really have gotten the drop on an experienced agent like Jim West?

Why not ask him?

As Jimmy Orlow continued to watch in fascination he suddenly realized that the Gunsmith was crossing the street towards him!

At first he felt excitement, then he started to feel panic.

Having no instructions on how to deal with this eventuality, he did the first thing that came to mind.

He ran.

Chapter Thirty

Clint ran after the boy and caught him after half a
block. The difference in their ages didn't seem to
give the boy any kind of speed advantage. He was
just flat slow!

Clint grabbed his shirt from behind and yanked,
practically pulling him off his feet. Next he slammed
him into a doorway face first, then turned him
around. Bleeding from the nose the boy stared at
Clint in fear and still some awe.

"What's your name?" Clint said, releasing his
hold on him.

"Orlow, J-Jimmy O-Orlow."

"You run with Jeremy Vincannon?"

"I, uh—"

"Come on, boy," Clint said, putting his hand on
the boy's chest, making him flinch, "don't make me
ask my questions twice."

"Uh, yes, yes, I, uh, I'm friends with Jeremy."

"Friends? Is that what you call it?"

Orlow didn't answer.

"Where is he now?"

"I don't know."

"Who else is he friends with, besides you, your
brother, and Dave and George?"

"My brother F-Frank..." Jimmy Orlow began,

and went on to name the others: Garrett, Granger and Fry.

"That makes eight of you?"

"Yes."

"You're sure that's all?"

"T-That's all I know of."

"And what's Jeremy planning?"

"H-He wants to make Chance Awakening into a town, a real town."

"With him in charge?"

"With all of us in charge."

"And then he'll build it up and systematically loot it."

"No!" Jimmy Orlow said. "We'll just . . . control it, we won't . . . won't *steal!*"

"You don't think so, huh, Jimmy? How old are you?"

"Eighteen."

"You didn't learn very much in eighteen years, did you?"

With a spurt of boldness Jimmy said, "I learned enough."

"Yeah, you learned to run with the wrong crowd. Tell me something, where are all the missing people?"

"What?"

"The people that you and your friends have either captured or killed, including two agents of the United States government. Where are they?"

"I-I don't know what you're talking about . . ." Jimmy Orlow stammered.

"You don't, huh? You know, for a bunch of amateurs you fellas have done real well." Clint grabbed him by the shirt and pulled him out of the doorway, sent him staggering into the street, where he went sprawling in the dirt. "Maybe it's time somebody showed you how the professionals do it."

"W-what are you gonna do to me?" Jimmy Orlow stammered from his seated position on the ground.

"I should throw you in jail, Jimmy," Clint said, "but I'm not. I'm going to let you go back and tell your friends, and your big leader, Jeremy Vincannon, that they now have the Gunsmith to deal with."

Orlow blinked at Clint, as if he couldn't believe that he was being let go.

"Move!" Clint shouted, and the boy jumped to his feet and ran down the street as fast as he could.

Clint had almost gagged on the word "Gunsmith," but he was trying to scare as many of Jeremy's followers as possible into walking away from him.

He was trying to save their lives, because if all eight of them came after him, he was not going to be able to do anything but try to kill them.

He didn't want to kill them, but he certainly wasn't willing to trade any of their lives for his.

Jimmy Orlow couldn't find Jeremy Vincannon, but he did find his brother Frank on the street. He ran to him—ran *into* him—and hung onto him while he caught his breath.

"What the hell is wrong with you?" Frank asked. "You're supposed to be watching the hotel."

"A-Adams—" Jimmy stuttered, "Adams caught m-me—"

"What do you mean he caught you—is that what happened to your nose?"

"To hell with my nose, Frankie!" Jimmy said. "He could have killed me."

"But he didn't. What did he say, Jimmy? What did he want?"

"He wanted us, and Jeremy, to know that he's coming after us."

"*He's* coming after us?" Frank Orlow asked. "There are eight of us, Jimmy."

"Frank, this is the goddamn *Gunsmith* we're talking about, not some traveling merchant. *The Gunsmith is after us!*"

"Calm down, Jimmy," Frank said, "calm down. We'll find Jeremy. He'll know what to do."

"Jeremy's the one who got us into this, Frank!" Jimmy pointed out.

"Yeah, well," Frank said, "he knew how to do that, all right, he'll know how to get us out of it."

Chapter Thirty-One

At first Derek Vincannon refused to involve his daughters, but Clint insisted that they might know something that could help, even if they weren't aware of what information was valuable. In the end Vincannon agreed to let Clint speak to them, and brought him to the house. Jeremy wasn't there. It might have simplified matters if he had been.

"Where's Jeremy?" Vincannon asked his wife.

"I don't know," she said. "He left to see about the shooting. He knew I was worried about you—"

"He never came to me," Vincannon said.

"Where did he go?" she asked, looking worried.

"I don't know..." Vincannon said. He turned and said to Mara, "Go outside with Clint. He wants to talk to you about something."

"Is he going to talk to me, too?" Melissa asked playfully.

Her father looked at her and said, "Yes, after your sister."

Melissa looked pleased, and eyed Clint, slyly running her tongue around her lips.

"What is it about—" Julia Vincannon started to ask her husband, but Clint didn't hear the rest of the question, or the reply. He allowed Mara to precede him, then followed her outside.

"What is it?" Mara asked. "Is something wrong?"

"Yes," Clint said, and told her everything he suspected about her brother.

"I knew he'd get into trouble," she said, "but I never thought it would be this serious."

"Why did you know?"

"Oh, the way he gathered that crowd around him, the way he talked to the shop owners, about things changing around here if they'd listen to him. He was always talking behind Father's back."

"Why did none of them ever tell your father?"

"I think a lot of them just never took him seriously," she said.

"And you?"

"I'm afraid I never took him serious, either."

"Mara, your brother may be holding some people who I'm looking for. If he is, where would he hold them?"

"How would I know?" she asked, with a surprised look.

"Maybe you don't *know* that you know," he said. "Just think a minute. Something he might have said, or something you might have seen."

"Are you going to ask Melissa this?" she asked.

"Yes."

"She may be able to give you the answer more than I can," Mara said. "She used to follow Jeremy without his knowing it."

"Why?"

"She was bored. She gets bored very often and looks for . . . things to do."

The tone of her voice and the look on her face told him that she knew about him and Melissa. Whether or not Melissa had told her he had no way of knowing.

"I'll tell her to help you," she said.

"She wouldn't otherwise, you mean?"

"She's playful, Clint, like a child, sometimes, even though she looks like a woman. She might decide to make a game of it, trade you something for the information. I'll tell her to help you without playing games. I'll send her out."

"All right, Mara," he said. "Thank you."

Mara nodded and went inside. Moments later Melissa came bounding out.

"What's the matter?" she asked. "Big sister didn't satisfy you?"

"I don't have time for games, Melissa—"

"Is that what last night was to you?" she asked. "A game?"

"No, it wasn't a game," he said, "and neither is this."

If she knew something he was going to have to get it out of her now. It was getting dark, and soon it would be too dark to search for Kate O'Hara and Jim West.

"Did Mara tell you what I wanted?"

"No, she just told me to help you. She's bossy sometimes."

"Just keep quiet and listen for a moment," he said, and then told her everything he had told Mara.

"Jeremy? Wants to take over?"

"Does that surprise you?"

She thought a moment, then said, "Well, no . . ."

"Then what?"

"I just don't think he's smart enough."

"He may not be, but he's smart enough to do some damage, and we want to avoid anymore. Do you know anything, Melissa?"

She played with the dirt with her toe and said, "I might."

"Melissa—"

"Well, we should trade!" she said, defiantly.

"This affects everyone in the settlement, Melissa," he said, warningly.

"I hate this settlement, Clint," Melissa said. "Do you think I care? I want something for me!"

"All right," he said. "What?"

"I want another night like last night, before you leave."

"That's all?"

She smiled and said, "You thought I was going to ask you to take me with you, didn't you?"

He didn't answer.

"Well? Do we have a trade?"

"We do," he said. "What do you know?"

"I know where you can start looking . . ."

It took a while but the Orlow brothers finally found Jeremy Vincannon, with Dave Hopkins and George Fredricks, in an abandoned building that used to be a trading post in the center of town. They were passing around a bottle of whiskey.

"What happened to your face?" Jeremy asked Jimmy, turning it first to one side and then the other to examine it.

"Adams," Frank Orlow said.

"What about him?"

Jimmy told Jeremy about his altercation with Clint Adams and Jeremy listened intently, taking a drink from the bottle every few seconds.

"That does it," he said, finally. "We've got to get him before he comes to us." He turned to George

Fredricks and said, "Find the others and then meet us at the livery. We'll pass out the weapons from the sheriff's office."

"Right," Fredricks said.

"What about us?" Frank Orlow asked.

"We'll go to the livery and wait. Once we're all properly armed we'll go and find Adams and do what has to be done."

"Out in the open?" Dave Hopkins asked.

"You worried about what your daddy will think, Davey boy?" Jeremy asked. "It's about time the people of this settlement woke up, anyway—and we'll give them the fireworks to wake up by."

Melissa told Clint that there was an abandoned building that Jeremy and his friends used to meet in, at the southern end of town. He wouldn't be able to miss it, she said. It was an old livery stable.

Clint walked to the south end of town and found the building. By this time it was dark, and he approached the building with caution, just in case someone was inside.

He saw no light from the outside, but still moved to the side door quietly. He found it unlocked and entered. The inside was pitch-black and he stood stock-still for a few moments, listening. Finally he was convinced that no one was inside.

He knew that lighting a lantern could give him away from outside, but he needed some light to search the place. He groped around until he found a lantern hanging on a wall, and lit it.

He saw the empty stalls, the dusty blacksmith's kiln, as well as some dust-covered tools. Hurriedly, he went through the stalls, not knowing what he was looking for. When he was finished with them he went back to the office. Just outside the office, inside a feed bin, he found all of the rifles and shotguns that had been removed from the sheriff's office. From the looks of them they had been in there a while, and had not been cleaned in sometime. He had some doubts about whether most of them would fire or not.

He searched the rest of the office, then, and found nothing. He checked inside the desk, but the drawers were empty.

He was about to leave when he noticed something. As he walked across the wooden floor he noticed a hollow sound beneath some of the boards. He stooped over, put the lamp on the floor, and moved a blanket that had been spread over the floor. He found a hinged door with a small hole. He put his finger in the hole and pulled, opening the door. He held the lamp out and saw a wooden stairway leading down. Some of the boards had rotted through and he had to pass over them on the way down. When he reached the bottom he saw that he was in a tunnel of some sort. It looked as if it had been inexpertly dug. This might have started out as some sort of root cellar, but someone had expanded it. They had not, however, known enough to shore the tunnel up with beams. As badly dug as it was, it could cave in at any moment.

He moved along the tunnel and saw that there were two doors at the end of it. He started revising his thoughts. Maybe not a root cellar, maybe a secret storage place that the army had dug, for weapons or food. It wouldn't have worked too well for weapons, as it was too damp.

He moved to one door and saw that it was secured

by a wooden bar that acted as a boot. He slid it back and opened the door. Holding the lamp ahead of him, he entered.

He saw the woman seated in a chair, hands and feet bound, blindfolded and gagged, but the red hair —lank and damp but still firey red—was a dead give away.

"Kate O'Hara!"

He saw her head jerk at the sound of her name, and as he was about to go to her and untie her, he heard the footsteps over his head, muffled by the dirt ceiling, but there were enough of them that he heard them.

Jeremy and his buddies!

Clint hurried back down the hall, up the stairs and pulled the door shut over him. There was nothing he could do about the blanket. If they noticed it and figured he was down there, then he was trapped.

He blew the flame out on his lantern and settled down there in the dark to listen, and wait.

Chapter Thirty-Two

Their voices were fairly clear and from the hole in the door he could see the light from their lanterns. It wasn't very bright, which meant they hadn't entered the office. He heard a door open, though, and assumed that they were looking in the feed bin.

"Who wants the shotguns?" he heard Jeremy Vincannon's voice ask.

A couple of voices answered and he couldn't identify them.

"The rest of you take rifles. You do know how to use these, don't you?"

There were replies of "yeah, sure," and "of course," which didn't sound very convincing.

They were amateurs for sure, but if they guessed he was down in the tunnel he'd be at a distinct disadvantage. If he was going to have to face them, he preferred to do it out in the open.

"All right," Jeremy said, "we're all armed, now let's find that bastard, Adams."

"You want me to check on the people downstairs?"

"What for?" Jeremy said. "The government man ain't going anywhere for a while, the girl's trussed up, and why worry about the kid? Let's go and find Adams and get this over with."

The light that he saw through the hole faded, and

he heard their footsteps as they all hurried out.

And then it was quiet.

He lit his lamp again and went back down the hall to the room, where Kate O'Hara was tied up.

"Kate," he said, kneeling next to her, "it's Clint Adams."

For the first time he saw an empty tin plate and some utensils near her chair, so apparently they were feeding her. Maybe she'd have enough strength to stand and move around.

He took off her blindfold first and she squinted at the light given off by the lantern. He reached over and lowered it. He took off her gag next and she said, "Clint!" breathlessly.

"Take it easy," he said. "Let me get you untied and we'll get you some water."

He worked on her bonds, freeing her hands and then her feet. She began to rub life back into her hands as soon as she was loose.

"Can you stand?" he asked.

"In a minute," she said, and started massaging her ankles.

"There are other people down here," he said.

"I know," she said, "but I don't know where."

"There's only one other door," he said. "I'll be right back."

He took the lamp, leaving her in darkness, and .went out of the room to another wooden door and opened that one. Holding the light high he saw two pallets with two bodies on them. One appeared to be a small boy.

He moved closer and saw that the man was manacled to the wall, the boy merely tied up. Both were either asleep or drugged. He shook the man a few times, then the boy, and decided that they were drugged.

He left the room and went back to Kate, who was standing.

"How do you feel?" he asked.

"Weak," she said, "but a hell of a lot better." She looked at him and said, "Am I glad to see you."

"Under other circumstances, I'd take that as a compliment."

"Who else is down here?" she asked.

"There's a boy in the next room, drugged from the looks of it."

"And?"

"And a friend of ours."

"Jim?"

Clint nodded.

"Is he . . ."

"He's alive," Clint said, "but apparently drugged, and manacled to the wall."

"Is that all?" she asked.

He knew what she meant. There were nineteen missing people, and the only one they'd found was the boy, the only child who was among the missing.

"That's it," Clint said. "Just the boy."

They stood there and let the implications hang in the air between them.

"I can't wake either one of them," Kate complained.

"It's just as well the kid's asleep," Clint said. "By the time he wakes up maybe we'll have him out of here."

"What about Jim?"

"We'll just have to take care of this without him," Clint said.

"Do you have a spare gun?" she asked.

"Not on me," he said, "and I don't think we have time to go and get one from my saddlebags. Wait a minute."

"What?"

"Let's go upstairs. I may be able to get you one sooner than you think."

They went down the tunnel to the steps and up into the livery office.

He saw that she was breathing hard and asked, "Are you up to this?"

"I'll be all right," she assured him.

"Let me look for that gun."

On the feed bin they found two rifles and a shotgun.

"Which do you prefer?" he asked.

"The rifle."

"Take the shotgun," he said, taking out a double-barreled Greener. "It'll be more effective, even with a near miss."

"I don't miss," she said.

He looked at her hands, which were shaking slightly, and said, "Not under normal circumstances."

She stared at him, then said, "All right," and reached for the shotgun.

"Not yet," he said. "Let me do a quick cleaning job while I tell you what we're up against."

When he was finished cleaning the shotgun and making sure it was in working order he handed it to her. There were also shells in the feed bin and he took out a handful and gave them to her.

"So we're facing maybe eight amateurs," she said, "with superior firepower and manpower."

"It's also dark and they know the area and we don't," he added.

"That's just fine," she said. "And what are our advantages?"

He was about to say, "We've killed people, already," but then he remembered that they had, also.

"I don't know that we have any clear advantages," he said. "The only one I can see is that we've been through this before."

"Their knowledge of the area and superior numbers might make up for that," she said.

"That's right, Kate," he said, "look on the bright side."

She was beyond responding to humor.

She broke the shotgun open, inserted two shells, and said, "Shall we get this over with?"

Both her tone and the look in her eyes were fierce.

"There's just one thing, Kate."

"What?"

"I'd like to take at least one of them alive," he said. "We need some kind of explanation for all this, don't you think?"

She was disheveled, undernourished, shaking . . . and angry as hell.

She snapped the shotgun closed viciously and said, "I could live without it."

Chapter Thirty-Three

They left the livery and stepped out into the night. Clint gave Kate a chance to take some fresh air into her lungs.

"Ready?"

She exhaled and said, "I'm ready."

"They'll be looking for me, which means they'll probably be inside the fort. Let's start there."

"Right," she said. "Lead the way."

Andy Fry kicked in the door of the guardhouse and Jeremy entered first, followed by the others, all holding their guns ready.

"Look in the back," Jeremy instructed, and the Orlow brothers went to do that.

"He's not there," Frank Orlow said, as they came back into the room.

"Did he pull out?" Dave Hopkins asked, sounding hopeful. If Adams left they wouldn't have to deal with him at all.

"His gear is still there," Frank Orlow said.

"He's still here," Jeremy said, looking at Dave. "It's not going to be that easy, Davey boy. Come on, let's go."

"Where do we look now?" Fredricks asked.

Jeremy grinned tightly and said, "My father's house."

The others couldn't believe it, but they followed him across the compound.

"Kick it in," Jeremy told Fry.

"But it's your house," Fry said, his tone puzzled. "You could just walk in."

"If he's in there I don't want to give him any chances," Jeremy said. "Kick it in."

Fry looked at the others, then shrugged and kicked the door open.

Clint and Kate were about to enter the compound when Clint saw the group of men crossing over to the Vincannon house.

"Back!" he said to Kate, and then ducked out of sight. He peeked around and watched as one of the men kicked in the door to the house.

"He's crazy," Clint said.

"What?" Kate asked.

"Jeremy Vincannon," Clint said. "He's mad. He just had one of the men kick open the door to his own house."

"Maybe we should be waiting for him when he comes out," Kate suggested.

Clint looked at her, nodded, and said, "Maybe we should."

"What the hell are you—" Derek Vincannon began.

"Be quiet!" Jeremy snapped. "Where's Adams?"

"Jeremy, what—" his mother began, but he ignored her. He went up to his father and asked again.

"Where is Adams?"

"I don't know."

"Don't lie to me!"

Derek Vincannon's jaw stiffened and suddenly he backhanded his son across the face.

"You . . . go . . . to . . . hell!" he said very deliberately.

Jeremy's head rocked back, but he stood his ground. His lips had split and he licked the blood away.

"That was probably your last official act as leader of this settlement," he said to his father.

"The others won't follow you," Derek said.

"They'll follow whoever has the power," Jeremy said, "and as you can see, I have the power."

"You mean you have the guns," his father said, "and these other cowards to back you up. That doesn't mean that you have the power."

"After I've killed Clint Adams I will."

Mara and Melissa came down the stairs, saw what was happening and remained silent, watching.

"Now, I need to know where Adams is."

"Go to hell."

This time it was Jeremy who backhanded Derek, whose head rocked back. As Derek moved to retaliate Jeremy shoved his pistol into his father's belly.

"Go ahead," he said.

Clint was looking in the window while Kate covered the door. He saw Jeremy strike Derek, and he could see by the look on his face that the elder Vincannon was not about to take that, even with a gun stuck in his belly.

He was going to get himself killed.

Before Derek Vincannon could do that Clint used the butt of his pistol and broke the glass on the window, then ducked back.

As the glass broke Jeremy whirled towards the window and fired his gun. The others followed, and soon the room had erupted with gunfire, all directed at the single broken window, which had now been obliterated.

Derek Vincannon grabbed his wife and pulled her to the floor, and shouted to his daughters, "Get down!"

"Stop firing!" Jeremy shouted.

They all stopped.

"Reload," Jeremy said, keeping his eye on the window.

"Jeremy," Julie Vincannon said from the floor, "what is happening?"

"Simply a changing of hands of authority around here, Mother."

"Jeremy," Dave Hopkins said, "he's outside."

"I know that, stupid."

"But . . . but he's waiting for us."

"I know that!" Jeremy snapped. He looked at his men and said, "George, take Steve and Wayne and go out the back. Circle around to the front."

"Right, Jeremy."

"Fry, go upstairs to one of the front windows. You're going to cover us when we go out."

"Right," Fry said, and went upstairs.

"Let me know when you're in position!" Jeremy called after him.

"Then who goes out?" Hopkins asked.

"The four of us are going out the front door," Jeremy said, looking at Hopkins and the Orlow boys.

"We'll get killed!" Hopkins said.

"Maybe some of us," Jeremy said, "but one of us will get him."

"Dave is right, Jeremy," Derek Vincannon said, standing up. He put his hand on his wife's shoulder, signaling her to stay down.

"What?"

"You're dealing with a professional gunman here," Derek said, "not some traveling merchants."

"What are you saying?"

"Adams told me about the missing people. Did you kill them all? Could you be that . . . that sick?"

"They had to die," Jeremy said. "They were coming here, outsiders. If they found out—"

He stopped short and looked away from his father.

"Found out what? What's so important that nineteen people had to die?"

"Eighteen," Jeremy said. "We didn't kill the boy."

"A child?" Julie said, in disbelief. "You have a child . . . hidden somewhere?"

"He's safe enough."

"And the government people?"

"They're alive," Jeremy said.

"Why keep them alive? They're more of a threat—"

"I might have to use them for leverage, to make a deal."

"A deal for what?"

"Just in case things went wrong."

Derek spread his hands and said, "And you don't think things have gone wrong?"

"All I have to do is get rid of Adams," Jeremy said.

"And you don't think the government will keep sending people," Derek said, "and keep sending people, and then finally send the army?"

Jeremy looked confused.

"Don't tell me that you expected they'd eventually stop sending people?" Derek asked, in disbelief. "With all your planning you couldn't be *that* foolish."

There were three thumps on the ceiling from above. Fry signaling that he was in position.

"Just stay out of the way, Father," Jeremy said, "and keep Mother and the girls out of the way."

"You're going to get killed, Jeremy," Derek said.

Jeremy glared at his father and said, "And that saddens you, huh?"

"It does."

"You should have *given* me some authority around here, Father," he said, "but you never did, you never shared—and now I have to take it!"

Derek looked at the other men and said, "If you follow him he's going to get you all killed. He's not a true leader. He's foolish and headstrong. Surely you've seen that—"

"That's enough!" Jeremy snapped at his father. He turned to face the other three men and said, "Get ready men. We're going out."

Frank and Jimmy Orlow exchanged glances, and then lowered their rifles.

"We're not going, Jeremy," Frank said.

"What?"

"You heard him," Jimmy said.

"You cowards!"

Jeremy turned and glared at Dave Hopkins. It had been Hopkins who had supplied the drugs that were keeping Jim West unconscious. He had taken them from his father's office.

"Dave?"

"You did the killings, Jeremy," Hopkins said.

"You and the others, George, Andy, Wayne and Steve. We didn't have nothing to do with those."

"What about the rape?" Jeremy said, reminding him. "When we raped the boy's mother we all took part in it."

"My God!" Julie Vincannon said, covering her mouth and looking at her son in horror.

"We'll all hang for murder if Adams gets away," Jeremy said.

"I'm not going out with you, Jeremy," Dave Hopkins said, and lowered his rifle.

That was when Jeremy killed Dave Hopkins.

Chapter Thirty-Four

When Clint and Kate heard the shot from inside the house they got ready for the men to come either from behind the house or from inside.

Kate was covering the door. With her shotgun she'd be particularly effective against a group of men coming out the door, huddled together.

Clint had taken a position further back from the house. Someone would surely come from behind the house, and not knowing from which side he had to be prepared to cover either side.

They both assumed that the shot was the signal that would start everything.

From the side of the house George Fredricks heard the shot and said, "Let's go."

From above Andy Fry heard the shot and broke the window with his rifle butt.

At the sound of glass breaking Kate swung her shotgun up and fired at the window. The buckshot caught Fry full in the face, nearly tearing his head from his shoulders.

As the three men came running from the left side of the house Clint fired. His first shot took the lead man, knocking him down. The other two men fired, but they were doing so in a panic and weren't even coming close. Clint fired twice more, before they could gain control of their nerves.

Outside the firing was over, but Clint heard several more shots from inside.

"Cover me!" he shouted at Kate, and ran into the house.

Inside he saw Mara and Melissa huddled together on the stairway. Three men were lying on the floor, obviously dead. One man—Jimmy Orlow—was sitting against the wall, clutching his side. Blood was leaking from between his fingers.

Derek Vincannon was standing over his son with a gun he'd snatched from the mantel.

"I killed him," he said, looking at Clint. "I killed my son."

"Derek—"

Julia came from behind him and put her hand on his arm.

"Jeremy shot Dave Hopkins," she said, "and then the Orlow brothers. He had only wounded Jimmy, and was about to kill him when . . . when Derek shot him."

"I couldn't let him kill the boy," Derek said, looking at Clint. "Do you see that? He'd been responsible for too many deaths, already."

"I see that, Derek," Clint said, taking the gun from him. "Everyone will see that."

Chapter Thirty-Five

The next morning Clint loaded the unconscious James West into the back of a buckboard that Derek Vincannon had given him. Dr. Hopkins had checked West and pronounced him healthy. He had been given too much of the drug that was keeping him unconscious, but should come out of it eventually with no lasting effects. Clint thanked the doctor and offered his condolences on the death of his son.

The boy was also riding in the buckboard, conscious, sullen, upset, incommunicative. Kate would sit with him back there, but it would take the boy some time to recover from seeing his mother raped, and both his parents murdered.

Clint drove the buckboard into the compound, where Derek Vincannon was waiting with his wife and daughters, and Kate O'Hara. The girls had supplied Kate with some fresh clothes, and she was bathed and fed and ready to travel.

Clint stopped the buckboard and stepped down. Kate hurriedly climbed into the back of the buckboard with the boy and West.

"The army will be here soon, Derek," Clint said. "I've already sent the telegraph message to Washington."

"We'll be ready," Derek said.

"It will be up to them to find out just what Jeremy was trying to protect here."

"What would your guess be?" Vincannon asked.

"It was pretty damp where they were holding West, Kate and the boy," Clint said. "If I had to guess I'd say that Jeremy somehow discovered a water source beneath the surface. Any kind of new source of water can be valuable. If it's not that, I don't know what it is, but that would be my guess."

Clint returned to the buckboard, then looked back at Vincannon again. Julie, Mara and Melissa were standing on the porch of the house, out of earshot.

"Talk to your daughters, Derek," Clint said. "Listen to what they have to say. You've got two children left. Make sure you don't lose them."

Derek nodded and said, "I've been a prideful, stubborn man for too long, Clint. I'll take your advice."

Clint extended his hand and Derek took it.

"Good luck with the army, Derek. Hopefully you'll be able to come to some sort of an understanding as far as staying here."

Clint climbed aboard the buckboard and looked into the back. Kate O'Hara had Jim West's head in her lap and one arm around the boy, whose name was Billy.

"Are we ready?" he asked.

"As ready as we'll ever be," Kate said.

Clint looked back at the Vincannons and wondered if it wouldn't be better for them if they didn't come to terms with the army, and moved on to someplace that didn't hold so many bad memories for them.